What the critics are saying...

"Another hot, hot read from the pen of *Jaci Burton*, *Midnight Velvet* is a sensual, erotic tale of mystery, betrayal, passion, romance and sensuality. With her usual finesse, *Ms. Burton* has created multi-dimensional characters, hot explicit sex and a fast moving plot. I read this book in one sitting and was squirming in my chair...I am a big fan of *Ms Burton's* work and she has not disappointed me yet." ~ *Valerie Cupids Library Reviews*

"*Midnight Velvet* is a thrilling adventure that engages the reader from the very first...*Jaci Burton* writes a suspenseful romance that readers will devour in one sitting. Charismatic characters, a gripping storyline, and red-hot sex scenes make *Midnight Velvet* a must read." ~ *Sinclair Reid Romance Reviews Today*

"Cops and Robbers is one of the classic games we all play as kids and one of the classic sexy plot lines that appear in romance novels. *Ms. Burton* takes the old formula and adds new kick in *Midnight Velvet*... The electricity between Tyler and Nevada is tangible and amazing. I love the way tensions of all kinds built to explosion and kept me so interested I finished this little diamond in a single setting." ~ *Keely Ecataromance*

"This book is all about action and suspense. If you love a good adventure story then this book is a must have. *Midnight* is intriguing and sexy; *Velvet* is adventuresome and perfect for *Midnight*... The love scenes are hot and intense with plenty of passion to keep the reader interested. *Jaci Burton* has created another wonderful story with plenty to keep the reader turning the pages until the very end." ~ *Angel The Romance Studio*

Jaci Burton

MIDNIGHT VELVET

ELLORA'S CAVE
ROMANTICA PUBLISHING

An Ellora's Cave Romantica Publication

www.ellorascave.com

Midnight Velvet

ISBN # 141995248X
ALL RIGHTS RESERVED.
Midnight Velvet Copyright© 2005 Jaci Burton
Edited by Briana St. James
Cover art by Syneca

Electronic book Publication March 2005
Trade paperback Publication September 2005

Excerpt from *Lycan's Surrender* Copyright © Jaci Burton 2004

Warning:

The following material contains graphic sexual content meant for mature readers. *Midnight Velvet* has been rated *E-rotic* by a minimum of three independent reviewers.

Ellora's Cave Publishing offers three levels of Romantica™ reading entertainment: S (S-ensuous), E (E-rotic), and X (X-treme).

S-ensuous love scenes are explicit and leave nothing to the imagination.

E-rotic love scenes are explicit, leave nothing to the imagination, and are high in volume per the overall word count. In addition, some E-rated titles might contain fantasy material that some readers find objectionable, such as bondage, submission, same sex encounters, forced seductions, etc. E-rated titles are the most graphic titles we carry; it is common, for instance, for an author to use words such as "fucking", "cock", "pussy", etc., within their work of literature.

X-treme titles differ from E-rated titles only in plot premise and storyline execution. Unlike E-rated titles, stories designated with the letter X tend to contain controversial subject matter not for the faint of heart.

Also by Jaci Burton

છા

Animal Instincts

A Storm For All Seasons 1: Summer Heat

A Storm For All Seasons 2: Winter Ice

A Storm For All Seasons 3: Sprint Rain

Bite Me

Chains of Love: Bound to Trust

Devlin Dynasty 1: Running Mate

Devlin Dynasty 2: Fall Fury

Devlin Dynasty 3: Mountain Moonlight

Dream On

Ellora's Cavemen: Legendary Tails II *(anthology)*

Kismet 1: Winterland Destiny

Kismet 2: Fiery Fate

League of Seven Seas: Dolphin' s Playground

Lycan's Surrender

Magnolia Summer

Mesmerized *(anthology)*

Passion In Paradise 1: Paradise Awakening

Passion In Paradise 2: Paradise Revival

Passion In Paradise 3: Paradise Discovery

Running Mate

Tangled Web

Midnight Velvet

Dedication

&

To Jamie and Mel,

who read this long, long ago.

Thank you for hanging in there with me and supporting
me when I needed it most.

To Charlie,

my partner in all things.

Thank you for always being there by my side and
encouraging me to reach for the stars.

I love you.

Chapter One

ဢ

If she didn't get some action soon, she was going to die of boredom.

Nevada James fingered the plants on her desk, trying desperately to think of some way to stay busy. She hated working the night shift. The small cubicle suffocated her and being an analyst was akin to a prison term. Dissecting coded information from the National Crime Agency's field operatives no longer held the thrill it once had. What she really wanted to do was become an operative herself.

Now that she'd received the letter informing her she'd been accepted into the field agent training program, her days as an information gatherer were all but over.

She smiled, anticipating the thrill and excitement of starting work with a seasoned agent. The commander told her he'd have her partner lined up by Monday, which meant tonight would be her last night as an analyst. Next week her new life would begin.

A call beeped in and she grabbed her headset, answering with her code name. "This is Velvet."

"Velvet? This is Midnight."

Ah, the voice of the mysterious agent known only as Midnight. She perked up at the sound of his husky tone, tightening her headset so she could hear him better.

Finally, relief from another boring night at the office. Her heart started its familiar race and for a second she almost forgot she was at work. Usually, taking calls from one of the NCA field agents didn't give her a moment's pause. That is, until Midnight called in. Then, the noise of the other analysts around her cubicle disappeared. It was just him and her. Alone.

His voice mesmerized her like a starlit sky at the witching hour, sending her libido into instant overdrive. The way he said *Velvet* made her wish it were her real name, instead of the code name the National Crime Agency assigned her. But he didn't know her name, nor she his. He was just a voice on the other end of the line. Safer that way in case their transmissions were tapped into.

"Go ahead, Midnight." Her fingers hovered over the keyboard, ready to take down the coded information. She entered his name and the time of his call. Ten-thirty p.m.

"It's hot out here, tonight, Velvet. How about there?"

Midnight's steamy voice conjured up images of a summer evening, the air still sweltering from the day's heat. Her mind filled with a vision of two bodies entwined under the stars, lips pressed against glistening, humidity-soaked skin. In St. Louis, almost every summer night was an experience like that. Only without the sexy part.

She broke into a sweat. "Yes, very hot." Why did talking to him always make her feel like a bumbling schoolgirl having her first conversation with a guy? She was twenty-six, not sixteen.

"So, are you ready for me?"

Did he have to lower his voice when he asked that? She knew he was supposed to make idle conversation in case the call was intercepted, but, God, did he have to be so good at it? "Oh, yes … I mean, go ahead."

"I'm trying to get an appointment with Mr. Smith but, so far, no luck. Maybe I can catch up with him tonight. I'll let you know if I get one scheduled."

With rapid keystrokes, she entered the coded message

and saved it for analysis later, though she'd already determined that Midnight's stakeout hadn't yielded any results yet. "Got it. I'll let the boss know."

"Thanks. You always give me what I need, Velvet."

Damn him. He sure made her feel sixteen. Nevada looked forward to these conversations, eager to hear his voice. It was always the same. He'd call and give her coded information along with some just-at-the-edge innuendo. She'd sigh and picture the two of them together, imagining how he might look. With that voice, he had to be hot. Her imagination conjured up a man a little over six feet tall, with dark hair and equally dark eyes. Tanned but not overly muscled. Kind of like a famous movie secret agent, only she doubted Midnight traipsed through the streets of St. Louis in a tux.

Silly as it was, she smiled into the microphone. Her fingers wound around a loose strand of her hair, nervously wrapping and unwrapping the tendril. She fought the urge to giggle.

"Got weekend plans?" he asked.

Not unless you've decided to kidnap me and have your way with me all weekend. "Not really."

"Oh come on, Velvet. Surely you have some hot guy tucked away."

In her dreams, maybe. "Um, no."

He laughed, a sensual growl that made her tingle all the way to her toes. She put her hand on her chest to still the raging thump of her heartbeat. She was certain anyone within fifty feet of her cubicle could hear it. "I'll give you a call when the meeting's set to go. You'll be waiting for me, right?"

One of these days he was going to make her explode right at her desk. "Of course." She was always a little bit sad when their calls ended. "Take care, Midnight."

"Later, Velvet." A click, and then dial tone.

She sighed, absently playing with a leaf on one of her desk plants.

"You've got it so bad, girl."

Nevada swung her chair around to face her eavesdropping coworker, Ellen Blair. "I do not." She pulled the headset off and brushed her hair behind her ears.

"Oh, please." Ellen rolled her eyes. "I listen every time you take one of his calls. I can't hear him, but I can hear you slobbering all over the phone. It's icky."

Ellen puckered her heavily glossed lips into an air kiss.

"Stop." Nevada was barely able to contain her laughter.

"No, *you* stop. I know he sounds hot and all, honey, but he's just a voice on the other end of a phone." She leaned over the waist-high cubicle wall separating their desks, her voice lowered to a whisper. "You need a real man, Nev. You *need* to get laid."

"No, I don't."

Ellen thought everyone needed sex as often as she did, which, according to her own accounts, was several times a week. Something about curvy blondes with baby blue eyes and long spiral curls must attract every man within shouting distance. Ellen was never at a loss for male companionship. The expensive jewelry she wore was proof of their adoration.

Petite blondes were in. Men rarely went for average brunettes like Nevada.

"You need it so bad you don't even realize it."

Ah yes, Miss Ellen the sexpert. "Think again. Besides," she shrugged, "I don't have the portfolio you do."

Ellen didn't even bother to blush, just brushed the expertly polished fingernails of one hand across her shoulder.

"You could have, if you'd ever try a real relationship instead of a fantasy one."

"A real one? Oh, I don't think so. Besides, you get all the guys, Ellen. I'm just an applauding bystander," she added with a wink.

Ellen shook her head. "You just refuse to see what everyone else does. I'd kill for your golden eyes and tanned skin."

"You're crazy." Nevada waved Ellen off.

"Anyway, you need to get out of your fantasy life and into a real, hot, shake-the-rafters, between-the-sheets romance."

Nevada shuddered at the thought. A real romance would be more than she could handle right now. Maybe ever. Her harmless flirtation with Midnight was right up her alley. Real was risky. As a fantasy, Midnight was the perfect man. In reality, she wasn't the least bit interested.

Besides, she'd soon have a new job and be too busy for romance.

The phone rang again, providing blissful distraction from thoughts of romance. "This is Velvet."

Static blasted in her ear. The call broke up so badly she could barely hear, but she recognized his voice immediately. His tone was sharp and clipped, not slow and lazy as usual. "Midnight?"

"I don't have much time. The meeting is on. Heading…now…but…car trouble…"

"What? I can barely hear you. You're breaking up, Midnight. Say again, please." The connection was terrible, but she caught the urgency in the screaming codes he yelled through the static.

"No time… blessings near the greens cemetery…have to…"

The phone clicked dead.

"Midnight!" She repeated his code name again, no longer able to quell the panic in her voice. Ellen whipped around the corner and hovered at Nevada's cubicle.

"Midnight, repeat message, please!"

Nothing. He was gone.

She posted the alert for an agent in trouble and hurriedly analyzed the codes. Something didn't make sense. His message only contained partial codes. She had to figure this out and fast so she could send an alert to the commander. Commander Alan Webster would get the ball rolling on Midnight's rescue. All she had to do was decipher the codes and try to ascertain his whereabouts.

Shit. She couldn't break the code. It wasn't right. There were integral pieces missing and without clear communication from Midnight, she couldn't figure out what he'd been trying to tell her.

"What's up?"

She glanced up at Commander Webster. He always looked so calm, even in a crisis. His brown eyes were like a pool of valium and she blew out a calming breath. "Emergency message from Midnight. But his codes don't make sense. I got no clear definition of his location, sir." She handed off the printout of her analysis and the commander took a glance.

He scanned the printout and frowned. "You're right. This doesn't make sense. Let me get some field people on it and we'll see if we can find him."

Field people. What she was going to be soon. She was already itching to jump out of her chair and find Midnight. If she could, she'd have flown out the door to go after him herself. That is, if she had any idea where he was. But field work wasn't her job. Not yet, anyway.

That's why she wanted to be an agent. This standing-by-doing-nothing part of her job drove her crazy. Why couldn't she be out there on the streets backing him up? Helping him? What if he was in danger? She'd heard that Midnight worked alone most of the time, something unheard of at the Agency.

"What happened?" Ellen asked in a hurried whisper as Nevada reclaimed her seat.

She explained the frantic call from Midnight.

"You're worried about him, aren't you?" Ellen asked.

"Of course I am," she shot back. "He's one of our agents and he's in trouble."

Ellen smirked. "Uh huh. And you've never taken a call like that before."

"I've taken lots of calls like that one."

"Exactly my point. And not once have I ever heard your voice raised in panic and fear. That called scared you, Nev. More than any you've taken before."

"That's ridiculous. I'm always concerned about the agents."

"Whatever you say, honey." Ellen harrumphed and returned to her seat.

Ellen might be right but it'd be a cold day in hell before she'd admit it. Of course Nevada was worried about Midnight. But more so than any other agent? Maybe just a little. His sexy voice did put him front and center in her thoughts. Even so, he was still nothing more than a voice on the phone.

* * * * *

Tyler Call hoped like hell that Velvet was good at her job. Otherwise he was fucked. Big time.

He'd just spent the better part of an hour hanging suspended from the undercarriage of a semi, which had finally stopped. Thank God. Now it sat in an old warehouse, with him still lying underneath it.

Damn the bastards who'd trapped him here. He'd just about finished planting the homing device when the driver had come out and cranked up the engine. He'd started to climb out but a couple men had exited the building, effectively cutting off his escape. He was stuck, an unwilling passenger on an unwanted thrill ride. Clinging to whatever his hands and feet could hold onto, he'd prayed he wouldn't fall off and wind up crushed under the truck's wheels.

And trying to make a call on his cell phone while balanced precariously underneath an eighteen-wheeler barreling down the highway should qualify him for stuntman status.

Failure? Not likely. Before today, anyway. This mission was heading in that direction, though. Time was running out and he had to escape. Lousy luck. This was supposed to be the easy part.

The mission was the most important thing. The only thing. As his father always told him, a Call didn't fail. When he was in charge of a mission, it succeeded. Period.

And now, trapped while a bunch of armed morons guarded the truck, it was obvious he had only one hope.

Velvet.

Thinking of her relaxed him. And worked him up at the same time. Every time she poured that sultry summer voice over him, the hairs on the back of his neck stood up. Among other things.

Great. Hell of a time to start thinking about a woman. That's why he never had relationships. Women took the focus away from his work and he wouldn't allow that to happen.

The call had been hard enough to make and being

outside as well as under a screaming truck hadn't done much to improve their connection. He'd barely gotten the call through before he lost the damn cell phone when the truck lurched. What a night. He was tired, hot, thirsty and pissed as hell.

And counting on Velvet. If she was good at intelligence, which he'd been led to believe, she'd gather enough information from his message to alert the commander to his whereabouts.

If she didn't, he was screwed.

* * * * *

One a.m. Nevada looked at the clock in her car and sighed. She was dead tired and finally heading home. She tried listening to the radio but flipped the power button after the first song, a haunting ballad about being lonesome.

Yes, she was. Just like every other night.

And now she could add worried to the lonesome part. She hadn't been able to get Midnight out of her mind. The rumors about his fate ran rampant around the office. They had no leads based on the codes he gave her. No one could find him.

Had she made a mistake in analyzing the code? Missed a vital clue that could have led the NCA to his whereabouts? She'd let Midnight down.

In his first call tonight, he said he'd set up a stakeout on a vehicle hauling methamphetamine lab supplies. She knew from the briefings that St. Louis was only one of a number of cities being invaded by a meth-producing organization. What Midnight had found so far indicated it was a centralized effort. Some organized group was responsible for the funding, creation and distribution of this lethal drug operation.

It was so quiet in the car she could hear herself breathe.

Her thoughts ran rampant over the clues Midnight had given her in that last frantic phone call, until something finally clicked.

That's it! Something about his running list of code words made sense, and it had to do with a church near a golf course and cemetary. She knew St. Joseph's neighborhood, had grown up there. And there was a golfcourse and a cemetery on either side of the street. That had to be the location Midnight referred to.

Under the freeway lights the exit loomed ahead. Without pause, she got off and headed for the old neighborhood. She always found comfort in the drive past her childhood house. It calmed her and reminded her how tenuous life was. If she blinked, it could all change. And it had.

It wasn't until she passed the ancient brick structure that she realized what she'd done. What possessed her to get off here? A nostalgia cruise brought about by Midnight's mention of St. Joseph's? Or a viable clue to his whereabouts?

As she drove past the abandoned warehouse where she and her friends had secretly played together as children, her foot slammed hard on the brakes.

Disbelief warred with certainty. It couldn't be this easy. Could Midnight have been referring to *her* St. Joseph's? The old church was only a half block from the warehouse. Not that he'd know it was her former church. But the more she thought about it, the more sense it made.

He'd said "green" too. The warehouse had green lettering on the sign at the front gate.

Coincidence? Maybe. Maybe not.

She shifted into park and took a quick peek out each side of the vehicle. Completely deserted. Who wandered around in a place like this at one in the morning anyway?

Maybe NCA field agents did. And she was *almost* a field

agent. Would be, officially, on Monday. She could almost hear the gears clicking excitedly in her head. What a great way to prove herself. Rescue one of the NCA's best agents.

No, Nevada. Dumb idea. Get back in your car, go to a pay phone and let the experts handle this.

Maybe if she sat a minute, really thought it out, this ridiculous Nevada-to-the-rescue idea would scatter. It didn't. And if she didn't follow through now that she was here, she'd kick herself all night. If she found something, she'd just run to a phone and call it in.

Simple, right?

She pulled up to the side of the warehouse and parked near the lower-level window. It looked deserted, exactly as it had been when she and her friends set up their clubhouse. Shattered, bar-covered windows stretched before her, the worn brick structure's five stories not nearly as imposing now as they had been to a girl of ten.

This is stupid. Go to a phone, call the agency and let someone else check it out.

But what if she was wrong? She'd look like an idiot, or even worse. Not a good first impression for a recently promoted field agent. Nothing like shouting fire and having the troops amass, only to discover an empty warehouse filled with nothing but rats.

Blowing out a breath to calm her nerves, she hooked her keys onto the ring outside her mini-backpack and got out of the car, slinging the backpack behind her.

She was leaving the car unlocked, in case she spotted something or someone. She wanted to be able to get in the car and take off as fast as she could. She might be about to become a field agent, but she was certainly no expert.

In the gloom of darkness, the place gave her the creeps. She was certifiably insane for even thinking about doing something like this. With a resigned sigh, she squatted down and peered in the basement window.

Nothing. Feeling more idiotic by the minute, she started to get up when a reflection in the window caught her eye.

Was that a light? Chills popped out on her arms and neck despite the still-lingering heat. She focused on that same spot and didn't have to wait long. There it was again. A flicker, a shadow of light. Fleeting, but there nonetheless.

It had come from the air vent across the lower level. The air vent leading to the underground structure. An oversized, empty room where she and her friends had played for hours. A quick crawl through the vent in the basement. She didn't dare risk going to the other side of the building and entering the lower level through the driveway. There might be someone on the other side. This side was dark and she could easily slip in without being seen.

She chewed her lower lip, knowing she should just go make a phone call, but something about the urgency of Midnight's call spurred her on. It wouldn't hurt to take a quick peek. She'd been in this place a million times as a kid. Chances were it was still as empty now as it had been then, so really, she was risking nothing by taking a look.

Maybe somebody rented the place and was in there working. So she'd go in and check it out. If it was nothing, she'd go home. If it wasn't, she'd get the hell out of here and make the call to the NCA.

The window was more difficult to open now than it had been sixteen years ago, but Nevada pulled with both hands until it gave with a creak. Thankful she'd worn her black capri pants to work tonight, she slid in legs first and slipped down through the narrow opening.

It was dark and musty. She wrinkled her nose at the stale air and brushed away the cobwebs tangling themselves in her hair. She felt her way across the room, using the old metal desk as her guide. It had been a long time but she still remembered the way. Only a few steps to the vent along the inside wall.

Found it! With a remembered sense of childhood intrigue, she pulled the screened cover off the air vent and climbed inside.

Just a short crawl to the other side of the vent. Mumbling prayers that she wouldn't run into any angry spiders in the long-unused tunnel, she slowly made her way to the end, careful not to make a sound. When she reached the mesh screen at the end of the vent, she was shocked at the activity in the supposedly empty warehouse.

An unmarked semi took up most of the space in the middle of the brightly lit room. She counted at least ten men loading some kind of lab equipment into the truck. What was going on? There were no cars parked outside the building. Her gut feeling told her no one was supposed to be in here.

Then again, it could be exactly as she thought. Some business had rented the old warehouse and she'd analyzed Midnight's codes wrong. Relief that she hadn't called in the big guns washed over her.

Her vantage point was limited because the vent sat at ground level. But the semi's tractor was perpendicular to her line of vision, giving her a clear view of the undercarriage.

She smothered a gasp as she spotted a man clinging to the underside of the truck. She couldn't see his face in the shadows, but the outline of his body was clear.

Now that sure as hell *wasn't* normal!

Was that Midnight? And if not, then who was it? Now what was she supposed to do?

Make the call. That's what she should do. The only logical option was to crawl out the way she came in, get to a phone and call the agency. She wasn't a field agent yet and could hardly defend herself with a tube of lipstick and a miniature flashlight.

Feeling ridiculous, she began to scoot backwards when suddenly the men closed up the back of the truck, turned out the lights and exited the room.

Pitch-black. She couldn't see a thing, not that she needed to in order to get out of the vent. Now what? Leave? What if the man under the truck was Midnight? Whoever he was, he was hiding from those other men. But was he the bad guy? Or were the others?

It had to be Midnight. Who else could it be? It made sense now, all of the codes he'd given her. She nodded in the darkness, more certain than ever that the man was an NCA agent.

And here she was, only a few feet away from him, poised to provide him a safe way out. How thrilling would that be? She'd be the one to rescue him. She'd already come this far. It didn't make sense to pull out now. Not when she could easily show him the way out.

But, how to get his attention?

The flashlight!

Maneuvering onto her side, she grabbed her bag, fumbling inside until her fingers closed around the cool metal of the tiny flashlight. She focused it against the vent screen, praying that none of the men she'd seen earlier were planted in the dark as guardians over the truck.

She flicked the switch on the flashlight. Nothing happened. She clicked it again, on and off, on and off. The battery was dead. Great. Now what?

She hesitated yelling his name on the off chance someone could hear her. Besides, what if wasn't even him?

Quit thinking that way. It is him.

As quietly as she could, she pushed at the mesh covering. It flew off with a loud clang. Nevada cringed at the sound, her body freezing to a standstill.

What to do now? That sound was loud enough to wake the dead, let alone the living on the other side of the door. Figuring she was already in the room, she quickly scurried ahead. She stayed low, crawling on her hands and knees, hoping she could remember the distance to the truck.

Throwing her hand out in front of her, she felt for the truck.

Almost there, just a few more feet and...

Suddenly she was on her back on the cold cement floor. A big, hard body had slammed on top of her. She was pinned! Unable to move. A prisoner. A small scream escaped her lips before a hand clamped down over her mouth.

His sharp whisper hissed in her ear. "Shut the fuck up or you're dead."

Panic rose like a bubbling pot. Her body shook with fear. Adrenaline pumped through her system, setting off a fight response. She kicked futilely against him, trying to wriggle free of the heavy body imprisoning her.

"Stop struggling!" His hand moved slightly away from her mouth.

She continued to fight, biting down hard on his hand.

"Sonofabitch!" he hissed.

When he jerked his hand away she opened her mouth and sucked in oxygen, readying her lungs for another scream, when sharp, cold steel pressed against her throat.

"You make one sound, you take a bullet."

She couldn't see a thing, but she knew that voice. Relief flooded her. "Midnight?" she whispered.

She heard his quick inhalation.

"Who the hell are you?"

"It's…it's Velvet from the Agency." Her voice quaked, not sounding anything like she normally did. *Please, please believe me.*

"Velvet?"

"Yes."

"Goddammit! What are you doing here?"

The terror began to subside about the same time he removed the gun from her neck. She took a few quick breaths and forced herself to calm down. "I was passing by on my way home. Your codes suddenly made sense. I know this place, and I…I thought I'd check it out."

He uttered a curse. "Of all the stupid, dumbass ideas."

He was right. It *was* stupid. But he could at least be grateful she'd come to rescue him. "Look, I understand you're upset. But if you'd just—"

The lights flipped on and she turned her head toward the front door to the warehouse. She saw feet. Running feet. A bunch of them. The familiar panic returned, only ten times worse. They'd been seen!

Without warning, strong hands yanked her up, pushing against her back. "Run!"

She literally ran for her life, Midnight right on her heels. She barely paused when she got to the vent and vaulted inside, scrambling on her hands and knees as fast as she could toward the opening into the basement.

They're coming! She knew it wouldn't take them long to find out where the vent exited, unless they were following behind them right now. All she could hear was the sound of her knees pounding against the metal of the vent.

She had already climbed the table under the window when Midnight came out of the vent. She pulled herself up, crawled out and headed to her car, reaching for her keys. Oh

God, her backpack! She felt around and looked on the ground beside her.

Midnight's feet crunched on the gravel behind her. "Get in the damn car!"

She stopped and searched the ground around her. Panic and desperate fear choked her. "My bag! I can't find it! My keys are in there!"

"What bag?"

"Tiny little backpack. Had my keys attached to it."

"What a fuckin' disaster." He muttered obscenities under his breath, shoved her in the passenger seat and ran around to the driver's side. Pulling what looked like a small metal hammer out of his jeans pocket, he slid into the seat and punched the ignition out.

A few seconds later, the engine roared to life. Thank God he was quick. She looked out the side mirror. Their pursuers were approaching quickly from the side of the building.

Hurry up and drive! She prayed they wouldn't be killed.

With tires screeching, he peeled out of the parking lot.

They had no sooner flown out of the parking area when she heard a series of loud pops. Oh dear God, please not a flat!

"Get down!" Midnight yelled. With a rough grasp he grabbed the back of her neck and pushed her head toward her knees.

"I thought that was a tire!"

"Not a tire," he said sharply as they drove quickly down the dark, deserted street.

If it wasn't a tire, then…"It was a gunshot! "They're shooting at us!"

"No shit! Keep your head down!"

She didn't want to die here. Not like this. Bile rose in her throat and she quickly tamped it down. *Not now. Deep breaths. Keep calm.* She tried to keep her inhales and exhales slow and steady.

After a series of careening turns and screeching tires, he said, "I've lost them. You can sit up now." His voice had calmed, but her nerves hadn't.

With her head buried against her knees and everything that transpired in the warehouse, she still hadn't seen what he looked like. It had been pitch-black in there, her sense of sight useless. And when the lights abruptly came on, she didn't even have time to focus before they ran for the vent. All she knew of him was his voice. She pulled her hair off her face and finally got a look at the man known only as Midnight.

Wow. Almost exactly as she had imagined. The streetlights outside illuminated hair the color of his code name. A couple days' growth of beard covered a strong jaw. He threw a glance at her and she sucked in a breath. His eyes were as sexy as his voice. Dark and forbidding.

"Do you have a cell phone?" he asked.

"Huh?"

His forehead wrinkled when he frowned. "A cell phone. You know, a telephone that goes with you?"

"I know what it is and no, I don't have one."

"Who in this day and age doesn't have a cell phone? Hell, even ten-year-olds have them."

"I don't." Who was she going to call with one? Her own voice mail? Then she remembered. "My bag! I have to have my bag!"

"Well you obviously don't have it or we'd have had keys to the car. Did you have it in the air vent?"

"Yes."

"How about when you crawled out of the vent into the

warehouse?"

She nodded, biting her lower lip, and then remembered. "I must have lost it when you threw me on the floor of the warehouse." Oh, God. She was such an idiot!

"Great. Just great." He quickly pulled into a convenience store, jumped out and made a call from the pay phone. He'd left the driver's door open; she could hear him arguing.

"Hey, it's not my fault she's here! Why the hell couldn't any of your people find me?"

He had to be talking to the commander. There went her field agent job.

Because she had no more business playing agent than a ten-year-old with a cell phone. Mortified, she sank into the seat.

"This is a joke, right?" He paced the length of the phone cord and back, sliding a hand through his hair. "I will not!" His brows furrowed in a way already familiar to her. "Like hell, I will!" More pacing, stretching the cord as far as it would go. "You've got to be kidding. Why can't someone else do it? I'm in the middle of a goddamn case here!"

After a long pause and a disgusted sigh, he shook his head. "You're the boss. But this is a really stupid idea." He ended the call abruptly. Without a word, he got back in the car, slammed the door shut and drove away.

She couldn't stand the silence for long, but was too afraid to ask about his phone conversation. "We don't even know each other's real names."

"So?" His lips clamped together and she could swear she heard him grind his teeth.

"My name is Nevada. Nevada James."

No answer.

"And yours?"

Still no answer.

"I guess I'll just continue to call you Midnight, then."

"Tyler Call."

Sexy name. She'd gotten a decent look at his body under the lights of the pay phone, and it more than matched her fantasies. Dark jeans hugged well-proportioned thighs, and broad shoulders fit snugly in his T-shirt.

"Are you taking me home?" She was tired, needed a bath and probably several glasses of wine. What a night it had been.

"I wish," he said with a caustic laugh.

Was he laughing at her? "What's so funny?"

He shot her a furious glare. "Funny? Not a damn thing is funny about this situation, Nevada-code-name-Velvet-James. You left your bag back there, which means your keys as well as your identification. By now, those men know where you live and where you work. They'll probably be at your place waiting for you. You're a witness to a crime. If they find you, they'll most likely kill you."

The thought of those men waiting at her apartment conjured up violent images that started her body shaking again. She crossed her arms, squeezing them tight.

Field agents don't fear, Nevada. Get a grip! "Okay. Now what happens?"

Tyler exhaled in a frustrated sigh. "Despite my opinion of this disaster, the commander thinks it showed initiative on your part."

She hadn't expected that and didn't even try to hide the smile that formed on her lips. "He did?"

He shot her a less than amused look. "Apparently."

"What does that mean?"

His hands clenched the steering wheel with a death grip

as he looked straight ahead. "It means I just became your training officer. And, for the time being, you're my houseguest."

Chapter Two

ဆ

Nevada swallowed, her throat gone dry. "Houseguest? What do you mean by that?"

Tyler didn't even look at her. "You heard me. And I don't like the idea any better than you do."

Oh, hell. Of course she couldn't go home. Her identification, keys, everything personal about her was in her bag. Thank God she didn't have pets or anyone at home waiting for her, otherwise they'd be in danger, too. Her little rented house and all her belongings were the only things she had. And if they got in and rifled through her things, a thought that made her shudder violently, they wouldn't find anything.

Except her NCA ID card.

She should have made the phone call.

"I don't understand. Why can't you take me to a hotel or a safe house instead?"

"Are you listening? I said you have to go with me."

She didn't know what to say. This whole night had been surreal. Why couldn't she have just driven home and left her dumb ideas in her head, where they belonged?

They drove for awhile, Nevada not even paying attention where they were headed. Finally, Tyler exited the freeway and turned down a dark road. She looked around at unfamiliar surroundings. They were well out of town, heading into a sparsely populated area. Where were they going?

This was too much. She couldn't get her mind around

what had happened in such a short space of time. First, she found out that she'd actually been assigned to a case. Okay, that part was pretty exciting. But to have to go home with Tyler? That part confused her.

"Any particular reason I have to go with you?" It sounded childish even to her. She didn't care. She needed time to think about all that had transpired. And she wanted to do that alone.

"Yeah, because our superiors ordered it. It's settled. Out of your hands now. Your little harebrained scheme screwed everything up. Nice job, *Agent* Velvet."

"Hey, that's not fair." Maybe she did screw up by going in when she shouldn't have, but he didn't have to be such an arrogant prick about it.

"Tough. Life's not fair. Neither's this job. Better get used to it."

Oh yeah. This was going to be fun. And she had to live with this guy? "How long do I have to stay with you?"

He flipped a glance in her direction. "Too damn long."

Now she was getting steamed. Being assigned to Tyler was the commander's idea, not hers. "I agree any amount of time is too much. But since I've been assigned to you, the least you could do is try to be pleasant."

"Yeah. I'll give that thought all the effort it deserves."

Which meant none at all. Maybe her desk job hadn't been so bad after all. And she'd fantasized about this moron?

More and more trees appeared along the side of the road, their density increasing the farther Tyler drove down the dark, deserted two-lane highway or road.

"Why aren't we going back to the agency instead?" At least there she could plead for a safe house or hotel. Anywhere but with Tyler Call.

"Protocol. Once an agent is compromised, you can't go

anywhere near the agency."

She groaned, wishing she'd driven straight home tonight. "This situation is not entirely my fault, you know."

He glanced at her. "Really. How do you figure?"

"If you hadn't grabbed me and thrown me down on the floor of the warehouse, I'd still have my bag."

"Uh-huh."

He wasn't buying it. How typical. Always the woman's fault. God forbid he should take blame for any part of this debacle.

"Tell me about your home. Any pets? Family members living with you?"

"No. I live alone."

He shot a glance in her direction. "Any lovers planning to come by this weekend?"

"That's personal." Not that she had any.

"No, babe. It's not personal. It's agency business. If anyone lives in or plans to stop by your house, the agency needs to know so they can arrange to intercept or rescue."

Oh. Mark two on her idiot's list. "No one. No family, no pets, no lover."

"Hmm. Interesting."

What the hell did that mean? If she wasn't boiling with irritation she'd push him further.

Before she had a chance to think of any more reasons she disliked Tyler right now, he turned left into a dense crop of trees. What was he doing? Did he live in the woods? Then she saw the almost non-existent dirt road. Cleverly hidden, the opening would easily be missed unless one was specifically looking for it.

The road snaked along forever before they came to a house. Actually, it looked more like a vacation home. Set amidst a wooded area thick with gigantic trees, the one-story ranch-style cottage was nestled dead center in the tender arms of Mother Nature.

Tyler pulled in front and stopped and they both got out. He walked past her without looking, pressing a button on his key ring that sounded three quick beeps. The lights inside the house came on instantly. An alarm system. She followed as he opened the front door and directed her inside.

It was sparse, with very little furniture and definitely bachelor decor. A large stone fireplace centered the small living area, which held a couch and a desk with a computer.

Off to the left of the entry was a kitchen complete with an early-garage-sale-style chrome and laminate table. Two matching chairs in the same icky yellow as the tabletop sat at opposite ends. Other than a few scarred walnut cabinets for storage and some old, greasy appliances, there wasn't much.

"You *live* here?"

"Sometimes, when I'm able to stand still for a minute." He walked away, leaving her in the middle of the living room.

Could this be any more awkward? He could at least show her around. Not much of a host, was he? Then again, charm didn't seem to be high on his list of qualities. Disgruntled arrogance ranked right up there, though.

She blew out a breath and looked around the rustic cabin, feeling out of place and thinking that perhaps she'd bitten off more than she could chew.

Not much she could do about that now.

Determined not to be treated like a piece of furniture, she followed him, but stopped dead when she realized he'd stepped into the bedroom. The only bedroom, from the looks and size of the place.

He'd removed his shirt and stood next to the bed, eyeing

her with impatience. She'd gotten a peek at his tanned, muscular back before he turned to her. And he was tall. Well over six feet would be her guess.

"What do you want?"

Did he have time for her to make a list? She tried to focus on the style of the furniture, the walls with no pictures, the door leading into the bath. Anything but his naked chest, covered in dark, curling hair that formed a V as it tunneled its way into the waistband of his jeans. *Oh, my.* "I want to know what happens now."

"I'm going to take a shower. You can do whatever the hell you want."

What did she want? She wanted to go home. Since that wasn't possible, he was going to have to give her more information. "That answer isn't good enough. I want to know how long I have to stay here and why I have to be at your house instead of a safe house or a hotel or somewhere else."

"Look, Velvet. This wasn't my idea, so I'm not any happier than you are about the situation we're in. I'm tired and I've got grease all over me from riding under that truck. I need a shower first, then a drink. So just go cool your heels and I'll answer your questions when I'm done. Unless you wanna follow me into the shower and ask them there."

Tyler suppressed a smile at the widening of her shocked brown eyes when he began unbuttoning his jeans. Was she going to stand there and watch him undress?

If she was, the twitch in his cock was going to be a helluva lot more in a few seconds.

Shooting him a scathing look, she quickly pivoted on one heel and scurried out of the room, shutting the door behind her.

Good thing, too. If she continued to watch him with that I'm-going-to-eat-you-alive look, he'd have had a hard time dropping his pants without letting her know how she affected him. He shook off the image of her little pink tongue sliding over her full lips.

He turned the shower on and stood under the warm spray, letting the heat and moisture linger on his stiff shoulders.

What a mess. First the mission and now Nevada.

Or Velvet. Whatever. Her appearance matched her voice, both exotic and smoky. Her long brown hair begged for a man's touch, as did her slender body. His mind strayed to images of sliding his hands around her waist, grasping that well-rounded bottom and pulling her against his heat.

Bad enough her voice had done things to his body. Now that he'd met her, his thoughts strayed to sex. Hot, nasty sex. Up-against-the-wall sex, his dick slamming into her sweet cunt until she screamed for him to make her come.

Nevada had attitude. And attitude made him hot. His desires strayed to confident, ballsy women, not fluffy little bunnies who'd cry the first time a guy looked at her sideways. She was the ballsy type. Hell, he gave her a ton of credit for taking the risks she had tonight to rescue him. Granted, it had backfired, but she wasn't afraid. And he admired a woman without fear.

Not that he'd ever tell her that. Because no matter how much he may have admired her guts, she was in his way. And considering it had been a long damn dry spell since he'd had sex, having Nevada underfoot was only going to cause trouble.

Because he sure as hell wasn't going to fuck her, no matter what his cock wanted.

He took his wayward hard-on in his hands and stroked it, the water and soap streaming down his arm to slicken his hold. No, he wasn't going to fuck her, but he could damn well jack off thinking about doing it.

She was petite, yet had womanly curves. Her eyes were amber brown, almond shaped and intense. He'd like to see those eyes turn a molten gold as he slid his shaft deep inside her pussy. She'd be a wildcat in bed, too, he just knew it. He bit back a groan as he imagined her full lips wrapped around his cock, sucking him as deep as she could take him.

Christ, he didn't want to come this way. Not when a woman whose mere voice could get him hard in seconds stood only a few feet from the shower. A woman he wanted to taste from head to toe. A woman whose creamy cunt would welcome his thick cock and squeeze the cum right out of him.

His balls tightened and he stroked faster, bracing his hand on the shower glass and tensed as his cock shot a hot stream of cum onto the floor. He breathed in and out steadily as his orgasm shuddered through him.

Hell, if masturbating while thinking about her gave him that powerful a climax, what would fucking her do? Kill him?

Shit. He shook the water out of his eyes and chided himself for his wayward thoughts. The idea was a hot shower, not a cold one, and if his mind kept straying to Nevada, he'd have to turn the water to frigid any second now. Better to focus on the mission and his next steps. First, he had to cover his tracks and fix the disastrous results of tonight's escapade.

After his shower, he threw on a pair of shorts and went in search of his new houseguest. He found her sitting ramrod straight on the couch, hands clasped in her lap like a bad student waiting for the principal to show up. Yeah, he'd like to treat her like a bad girl. Over his knee, panties down to her ankles and his hand on that fine ass of hers, giving her swats that would make her cream.

Focus, dammit.

When he walked in, she shot him that deer-in-the-headlights look, then quickly disguised it to one of irritation.

Maybe she wasn't as cool and calm as she'd led him to believe. "You can relax, you know," he said as he passed by to grab something to drink.

"I *am* relaxed."

Right. She was as calm as a cornered animal.

"Would you like a drink?" he called out from the kitchen.

"No, thank you."

Polite, too.

The bourbon and water would help him unwind before sleeping. Too many conflicting thoughts rolled around in his head right now, not the least of which was parked like a stone statue on his couch.

He flopped in a chair next to her. She looked over at him, sort of. Actually, she looked at him, the wall, the computer, the front door and the hallway. Then, every few seconds her eyes would dart back to him.

"You haven't looked at the ceiling yet." He hid his smile behind the glass.

Her eyes met his. Direct, golden and pissed off. "I'm not exactly thrilled to be here, you know."

"Why?" Though he already knew the answer.

"Why? Let's see." She began to tick off a list on her fingers. "First, we almost got killed. I lost my bag, my driver's license and my credit cards. It held the keys to my home, which is probably being ransacked as we speak. And to top it off, I'm stuck here in the middle of nowhere with a man who quite obviously doesn't want me around. I don't know why I was so stupid to think that the mighty Midnight might actually need my help. Yes, I screwed up, okay? And it cost me my freedom and for what? To be stuck here with an arrogant ass like you? *That's* why I don't want to be here."

And edgy. He leaned forward and held out his glass. "Take a drink. It'll help."

She looked at him suspiciously, but took the glass from his hand. He tried to ignore the punch to his gut as her lips covered the same spot where his had just been. She swallowed and handed the glass back to him. He fought the urge to lick that exact spot on the glass where her mouth had been.

"The agency has already cancelled your credit cards and put a watch on your apartment. If anyone tries to get in, they'll know."

"That's so comforting."

He sat back and watched her fidget. Finally, she stood and paced the room.

"Are you sure you wouldn't like a drink?"

He was shocked when she whirled on him, golden eyes flaming. "No, I don't want a drink! I don't want to sit here making idle conversation with you. I want to know what's going to happen next. What about my job? I was supposed to start a training program on Monday. A program I've spent a year trying to get into. I want to know how long I'm going to be here and how this affects my training. And what the hell am I supposed to wear? I need some answers, not a goddamn drink!"

Whoa. A spitfire lurked under that icy calm. He resisted the urge to smile, hoping to hell his cock would resist the urge to stand up and salute a woman with some spirit.

Shrugging, he answered her truthfully, which he was fairly certain wasn't what she wanted to hear. "As far as your job, quit worrying about it. The commander wants you to start field training first. Since you already tossed yourself, unwanted I might add, into this case, you're staying here to work with me. As far as the rest, I'd like to say I had all the answers for you, babe, but I don't. Sorry."

Her eyes flashed anger and her body language told him everything. She crossed her arms—protecting herself. She paced—nervous. She chewed her bottom lip—apprehensive. The woman was seriously stressed.

Maybe she just needed a little old-fashioned sex to calm her down. Yeah, right. The sex would be for him, not her. He was so aware of her right now his nerve endings were screaming for him to jump up and take her. Take her hard and fast and force her to turn that wild energy to something productive, like fucking his brains out.

He paused mid-drink and considered it, then just as quickly discarded the thought. *Just what you need to add to your list of major foul-ups today. Sex with someone who works for the agency. Idiot.* He needed to go to bed.

Alone.

"Well?"

"Well what?"

"What happens now?"

He yawned. "I have no idea. We'll figure it out in the morning after I've had a chance to do some reconnaissance."

"And in the meantime?"

"You stay here. With me. I protect you and train you— you continue to live. Pretty simple."

She looked over the walls, ceilings, doors and windows. "Are we safe here?"

"As safe as you can be. I have a security system that alerts me if anyone comes within one hundred yards of the house. Plus, a few little surprises should someone breach the perimeter. And I'll know if someone comes close. Trust me."

"Oh." Her gaze darted around the room, searching for hidden traps.

"Don't bother looking for them. You'd never see them.

No one can. That's what makes them effective."

"I'm not stupid, you know. I realize how security is structured. We work for the same agency, remember?"

How could he forget? That voice of hers was his lifeline on nights when he felt alone. She warmed him, made him feel things he shouldn't feel about someone he was supposed to protect. And now that he'd seen the face and the body that went with the voice, it was so much better than it had been in his fantasies. And worse. "Analysts don't get the same training agents do."

Her eyes narrowed. "Which still doesn't make me stupid. And besides, didn't you say you were my training officer? I was accepted as a field agent trainee. I have had intelligence training and I don't expect to sit here and be protected by you. I want you to teach me."

Feisty little thing. He admired her for that. She was in the wrong, had screwed up and she damn well knew it, and yet she wasn't going to give up. A point in her favor.

Teach her? Hell yeah he'd like to teach her a few things, none of which had anything to do with the agency. He blew out a quick breath to get his libido under control. Somehow he got the idea she wouldn't be very happy spotting his growing hard-on.

To start, he'd have to teach her some basic self-defense moves, if for no other reason than an added security measure. But not tonight. He'd been awake almost twenty-four hours and was dead on his feet. So was she, as evidenced by the dark circles under her eyes. Eyes he wanted to press his lips against, easing away her strain, her fear.

He stood abruptly. "I suppose we need to find you something to sleep in."

"That would be a good start."

He went to the bedroom and came back with one of his

T-shirts and tossed it at her. "This will have to do."

She fisted her hand around it. "Thanks. I need a shower, too."

He directed her to the bathroom, then sat on his bed and listened while the shower ran. Listened to the water running, imagined her slipping out of her pants and silk blouse. Sliding out of whatever undergarments she wore, which in his imagination were lacy, silky and utterly decadent.

He groaned, then decided he'd better think about the mission instead.

Thinking about work helped get his mind out of the gutter. Until she stepped out of the bathroom and into the bedroom, stopping at the foot of his bed. His old gray shirt was way too large for her and more seductive than if she'd been clad in a see-through nightgown. Her long hair cascaded in a dark waterfall, resting over small, well-shaped breasts outlined by the clinging, worn cotton. Her long legs tantalized him, peeking out from under the ragged hem of his favorite college shirt.

Her gaze swept to the thin sheet covering his hips. Then she looked into his eyes and licked her lips nervously before quickly looking away. He caught a brief glimpse of feminine awareness that made him ache and want to throw the pillow over his lap. Or throw her over his lap.

He tried not to groan. She was sex incarnate and he mentally cursed the instantaneous rush of desire.

Why couldn't she be twenty years older than him or ugly as hell? Just because she had a sexy voice didn't mean the face and body had to match, did it? And the feisty personality that went with the package fueled his interest even more. She had guts and bravado, he had to give her that. What a turn-on.

"Where do I sleep?"

A thought came to mind, but he cast it aside as a really bad idea. "You have two choices," he explained, mentally cursing his lowered voice. "In the bed, or out on the couch."

Damn if her eyes didn't immediately turn to the empty side of the bed. He squirmed under the covers. There went her arms, crossing in front of her like a shield of armor.

"I didn't mean in the bed with me. If you want the bed, I'll take the couch." Then again, maybe he should have waited until she decided.

No, Tyler. Bad, really bad idea.

"The couch is short and you're too tall," she said. "I'll take the couch. Could I have a blanket?"

He picked up one of the pillows behind him and tossed it to her. "There's a blanket on the back of the couch."

She lingered, clutching the pillow in a death grip, staring down at his crotch with a look so hungry it was physically painful. *Don't stay, walk out of the room. I'm strong, but not that strong.*

"Goodnight," she said in a near whisper.

"'Night." He turned and flipped off the bedside light, leaving her in the dark. Hopefully, she'd scuttle out of the bedroom before he did something really stupid—like kiss those oh-so-kissable lips of hers.

* * * * *

Nevada tossed, turned, flipped the cover off and then on again. She sighed, cursed quietly and threw mental daggers at the man sleeping soundly in the next room.

He was a terrible host.

This wasn't a slumber party, she didn't want to be here and damn him for making her feel like an intruder.

The pillow carried his scent. Dark and dangerous, a musky, sexy smell that fit the man perfectly. She sat up, punched it and flopped her head back down. Staring at the dark ceiling, she listened to the sounds of his rhythmic breathing. At least *he* didn't have any trouble going to sleep.

Not only had her life changed abruptly in the blink of an eye, but she was in an unfamiliar house, with no clothes and no personal amenities. To top it off, a sexier-than-hell man slept a few feet away. She had no earthly idea what was going to happen next. This kind of situation didn't set well with her at all.

Sleep wasn't coming. She finally gave up and propped the pillow against the back of the couch. More than anything, she wanted, needed to be in control of her life. Too many bad things happened when she wasn't.

She hadn't meant to screw up Tyler's mission—it had just happened. And now she was paying the price for risking her life to save a voice on the phone. Tyler "Midnight" Call would have been better left as a fantasy. Someone to play with in her mind, indulge her sexual fantasies, then put away in the deep recesses of her brain until the next time.

Her fantasies had conjured up a sexy, virile, movie star type of agent. Okay, maybe he was all that, but she also pictured him as gallant, caring, warm and loving. She snorted out loud at how ridiculous that notion was. And she didn't care if he heard. It was her fantasy, after all.

* * * * *

Tyler woke early, as usual. Not one to vary from routine, he rose just before dawn and planned a morning run. He threw on a pair of gym shorts and sleeveless shirt, grabbed his tennis shoes and headed into the living room.

The first rays of the sun peeked through the window next to the front door, casting a soft glow upon the woman asleep on his couch. He sat on the chair next to the couch to put on his shoes. Okay, mainly to watch her.

She was tangled up in the covers, one tanned and slender leg thrown over the blanket. His T-shirt rode up her thigh, lending him a vision he wasn't prepared to handle.

Her back faced him, her long dark hair a tangled mess. He resisted the urge to reach out and smooth his hand over her exposed thigh, but damn if he didn't ache to slide the cotton shirt up over her hips and caress the skin he knew would feel as soft as velvet.

He needed to get out of there.

Too late. She stretched and turned over on her back, raising one arm over her head. The shirt lifted over her hips. Of course, she just *had* to push the blanket off with the other hand.

He tried not to groan too loudly as he glimpsed the skimpy white string bikini panties barely covering her sex. Dark curls pushed out from the flimsy vee of the panties. He'd bet they'd be soft as silk to the touch. Maybe he'd just sit there for a while and watch her change positions.

No. Run. Don't think, just run.

This woman was a complication, a hindrance, he reminded himself as he tiptoed out the front door and headed down the steps to begin his run.

The mission was a mess, he had a million things to do and the last, absolute last, thing on his mind should be the sexy woman in his care. But sure as hell, that's where his mind wandered — over and over again.

He blew out a couple quick breaths and set into a run, hoping the oxygen would help clear his head. Following the trail he'd laid out years earlier, he concentrated on his pace, pushing, but not too hard. He filled his lungs with deep breaths of morning air, thinking of nothing but each step, each mile.

By the time he returned to the house, he was calmer,

more in control.

After his run, he stepped quietly in the house. Nevada was still asleep, so he started coffee, then showered and dressed. By then, the coffee was ready and it was time for Sleeping Beauty to rise.

"Hey," he said as he shook her shoulder. She moaned and slapped his hand away. "Nevada, wake up."

She turned one half-opened eye on him. "What time is it?" Her voice sounded way too morning-after sexy, which only irritated him since he didn't get to experience the night-before part.

"Almost eight."

"Ick. Go away." She pulled the covers over her head.

"How much sleep do you need?"

"More than what I got," she mumbled. "I was awake almost all night."

"I see. Well, the coffee's on. Nothing in the fridge to eat since I haven't shopped yet, but I'm sure you can find something in the pantry. I'm going out for awhile."

She waved a hand at him. "Yeah, okay. Bye."

He shook his head, grabbed his keys and left. After retrieving his SUV, he headed down the driveway, pushing buttons from the hand-held security device that activated the perimeter system. His houseguest would be safe.

First things first. He'd have to see about getting said houseguest out of his house, and out of his life. He was an agent, not a bodyguard. Or a trainer.

God. He couldn't believe he had to field train a new agent. Like he had time to hold her hand and watch out for her while he was trying to do his job at the same time. What a mess. This whole scenario could royally screw up his mission.

No, it wouldn't. He just wouldn't let it happen. When he had a mission, the mission always came first.

The sexy agent wannabe would just have to take a back seat for now.

Chapter Three

ॐ

Nevada's back ached from what little sleep she'd managed on the couch from hell. In addition, she needed a comb, a toothbrush, other personal items and some clean clothes. And there was no food in the house.

Obviously, Tyler was trying to kill her. He was so angry with her about last night, he'd decided to abandon her until she starved to death.

She vaguely recalled a conversation with him earlier, but how much earlier she couldn't recall. The clock read noon and she'd been up for an hour, scrounging through the pitifully barren kitchen cabinets in search of something edible. The only things she found were saltine crackers and some cheese in a jar. Just what she wanted for breakfast.

At least it was food. She wandered around the house, dropping a trail of cracker crumbs behind her like Hansel and Gretel.

The house was small, just one bedroom and bath, kitchen and living area. A tiny computer desk sat against the wall in the living room, presumably where a television would have gone, if there'd been one. No TV, no radio, no sound. Not a single book or magazine in the place and she'd looked everywhere.

Sensory deprivation, another form of torture. He *was* starving her to death, depriving her of both biological and sensory sustenance.

Nevada giggled. Her mother had always called her a drama queen and she'd certainly made a soap opera out of her current state. She should feel lucky to be alive at all under the circumstances.

If she didn't have anything to watch, listen to or read, she'd just have to find something else to do.

She passed by the back door. Last night it had been too dark to look outside. When they'd arrived, the thick woods blocked her view of everything but the little house in the clearing. She pushed aside the tiered curtain covering the back door window and a wonderland opened up before her eyes.

The house sat on the edge of a gorgeous, blue lake!

She'd always loved the water, eagerly anticipating summers with her parents. Summer meant camping, swimming and boating, then roasting marshmallows at night and sleeping under a starlit sky.

But that was when she was still little. Before her mother's illness took her away too soon and her father's complete withdrawal into alcoholism took him to a place she couldn't reach. His death a year later left Nevada without a single living relative. Two deaths within a year, neither of which she could prevent.

She shook off the memories and opened the back door, hoping the sunshine and fresh air would clear out the dark cobwebs of the past.

The heat was oppressive, sucking the oxygen from her lungs. She struggled to inhale a cool breath. The humidity was unbearable today and by mid-afternoon would be brutal. She longed to slip out of her T-shirt and plunge into the cool lake water.

Maybe she'd just go down and take a look, even put her feet in. There were large, flat stepping-stones leading the way from the door to the wooden dock and she followed them toward the water.

Beautiful. Secluded, not another house or dock in sight. Nevada sat at the end of the dock and dangled her feet in the cool water, debating whether to slide in with the T-shirt on or risk skinny-dipping. She looked around but couldn't see a thing. The tall trees, which by light of day were a mixed bag of oak, sycamore and birch, surrounded the lake. There were no other signs of life around her. No houses, piers, inhabitants, nothing to indicate Tyler had any neighbors within shouting or, more importantly, viewing distance.

It was so hot she began to sweat, the shirt clinging to her breasts. Tyler's scent permeated the shirt, a sweet musky smell that had more to do with the man and less with cologne. Part of her restless night had been caused by that seductive scent of his, and knowing a shirt he had worn touched her naked body.

Now she was really hot. Considering the underwear she wore was the only pair she had here, she made a quick decision. She hurriedly undressed and slid feet first into the cool water.

* * * * *

Tyler hadn't found out any more this morning than he'd known last night.

His friend Dylan Maxwell, NCA code name Legend, squinted amused blue eyes across the table. "Say that again? You were rescued by an analyst?"

Tyler knew he shouldn't have said anything, but Dylan knew as much about him as he'd allow anyone and he needed a professional ear. He'd just have to endure the teasing first. "I didn't need her to rescue me. She stumbled onto the place right at the time I was ready to make my escape."

"Uh-huh." Dylan took a bite of his sandwich and arched a knowing brow as he chewed. "You'd have gotten out all by yourself if she hadn't shown up, right?"

If Tyler didn't like Dylan so much he'd be pissed. "Yeah, I would. I saw the vent, figured it for an exit and waited for an opening to get the hell out of there."

Dylan leaned back against the café's chair, stretching his long legs in front of him. "Whatever you say."

Tyler pushed aside his irritation at the thought of being saved by Nevada. "Anyway, did you find anything?"

"No. The truck was gone by the time we got to the warehouse and hasn't been seen since. It's been moved to another location or maybe it's far out of town by now. And no sign of our elusive Smith either."

Tyler sighed. Smith was the code name for whoever was responsible for coordinating the biggest meth lab operation in the country. Every NCA division was on the lookout for him and Tyler had spent months monitoring the newest meth lab setup in his four-state jurisdiction. He thought he'd finally gotten somewhere by planting the homing device on the truck. By now, the beacon had most likely been discovered and destroyed.

Dammit all to hell anyway. If it hadn't been for Nevada showing up, he'd have been able to slip away unnoticed last night, the homing beacon firmly implanted on the truck.

"So, now what?" Dylan asked.

"Now it's back to square one, I guess. Try to find a link, a clue that will lead us to Smith." And in the meantime find a way to get out of his latest assignment of playing babysitter to Nevada.

"What's she like?"

"Who?"

"You know who." Dylan smiled and leaned across the table to whisper her code name. "Velvet."

"She's about like I expected." Hot. Sexy. Exotic.

"Too bad. Beaten with the ugly stick, was she?"

Tyler laughed. "Yeah, something like that." He'd be damned if he'd tell Dylan that Nevada was beautiful. Let him find his own girl.

Let him find his own girl. What was he thinking? Nevada wasn't his. Never was. Never would be. She was an assignment and nothing more.

But Dylan knew him well. "Why do I get the idea you're keeping the secret of Velvet to yourself?"

He shrugged. "No secrets to keep. I have to guard her, train her and hopefully dump her as soon as it's safe."

"You sound thrilled."

"You have no idea."

Dylan took a long swallow of tea and pushed his plate to the side. "If she's that inept, just tell the agency she's not field agent material."

Trouble was, she wasn't inept. What she'd done last night, while stupid, had shown guts and initiative on her part. He couldn't argue with the commander's assessment of the situation, because despite the inconvenience to him, gutsy agents were hard to find these days. She might be a greenhorn at field escapades, but he'd bet she was a quick study.

"It's not that bad. Bad timing more than anything."

"And maybe she struck a chord in you?"

"What do you mean?"

"Maybe she's not hideous looking, and…hell man, when was the last time you got laid?"

Too long to remember. The job had been keeping him busy night and day. "It's been awhile, but she's not my type."

"When you're desperate, any woman is a man's type," Dylan offered, waggling his eyebrows.

Tyler started to argue the point, but the shrill sound of his beeper shot him upright in the chair. He yanked it off his belt and scanned the alert code. The perimeter at the house had been breached! He cursed and leapt from the chair, knocking it over.

Dylan was beside him in a second, running. "Need backup?"

He nodded. "Follow me!"

They jumped into their cars and raced down the freeway. Fear tightened Tyler's gut at the thought of Nevada being in danger. He had to hurry!

The drive took way too long in his estimation, even though they'd only been on the road about ten minutes or so. Nothing seemed out of place when he pulled in front of the house and leaped out of the car.

He and Dylan tiptoed to the front door and opened it, guns drawn, checking it room by room. Nothing was out of place but Nevada was nowhere to be found. Where was she? Did someone break in and take her?

No way. No one knew about this place and no one trailed them last night. He was one hundred percent sure of that fact. So the alarm had to have been triggered by something else.

He ran out the back door, Dylan close behind. The first sounds he heard were the splashing noises coming from the end of the pier. He stopped suddenly and crept toward the water, crouching low and staying hidden in the shrubs.

Nevada was out there. She was alone, thank God. His heart hammering and the blood pounding in his head, Tyler leaned over and rested his palms on his knees in an effort to catch his breath. Dylan inched up behind him.

"What's going on?" he whispered.

"Nothing. She's alone. She must have set off the

perimeter alarm when she crossed the end of the pier to swim."

"So, she's okay?"

More than okay. Naked in fact, floating on her back in the middle of his lake. Hell and damnation if she didn't look like a water nymph, a siren beckoning him with her water-glistened body. He was too far away to see her in any detail, but close enough to feel the discomfort in his jeans.

He should be pissed as hell, but for the life of him, the only emotion he could muster was relief that she was unharmed. And a tingling sensation in his gut that had nothing to do with fear and everything to do with sex.

Dylan laid a hand on his shoulder to move him out of the way. "Let me take a peek."

Tyler whirled and covered the available peeking area with his body. "I don't think so."

"Oh, come on. She can't be *that* bad."

"She is. Trust me. And you just had lunch."

Dylan laughed, pushed Tyler aside and strode toward the dock. "Let's go meet your houseguest."

This was going to be uncomfortable. For everyone.

* * * * *

Nevada was in absolute heaven. The sun heated her skin as she floated on the water, naked as a jaybird and feeling freer than she had in years. She was probably going to be burned and blistered, but didn't care.

Reluctantly, she realized she'd spent enough time in the water and should sneak out before Tyler came back. The last thing she wanted was to embarrass herself in front of him again.

She did a few backstrokes and then dug her feet into the sandy bottom. After a huge inhale, she scrunched down under the water and mentally counted the seconds. She'd always been good at holding her breath—she wondered how long she could do it now?

Popping her head above the surface, she blew out the water she'd swallowed and swept her hair away from her face. Just one more minute and she'd get out. She smiled as she recalled thinking the same thing about ten minutes ago. But the water was so heavenly and what was she going to do in the house anyway? Count cracker crumbs?

But she'd better quit floating around before—

"Hey there, princess."

She screamed and quickly crouched down in the water, hiding as much of her nudity as she could. A man stood at the end of the dock. He was tall and dark, but definitely not Tyler. His build was a little different. She couldn't see his face because the sun was to his back.

"How's it going, Velvet?"

Who was he? And how did he know her code name? His back was to the sun, his face hidden in the shadows. But she knew the voice. Always the voice. "Legend?"

"Very good, darlin'. Nice to see you in the…ah…flesh. And some mighty fine flesh, too."

She'd have recognized that southern accent anywhere. Though she hadn't spoken to him as often as Midnight, Legend's voice was equally as memorable. Her face heated in embarrassment.

"Um, hi, Legend." Great. *How nice to meet you and how fortuitous that you showed up just as I was naked.* How was she going to get out of this one?

"Are you going to parade around naked in the lake all day or would you like to get out now?"

She cringed when she saw Tyler step around Legend. Oh God, they were both here. And she was…way more exposed than she wanted to be. "I just took a swim."

Legend relaxed his posture and crossed his arms. "Go right ahead and swim, honey. I'll just stand guard."

"I don't think so," Tyler said. "Go check out the perimeter."

Legend shrugged. "Oh sure, have all the fun yourself." He saluted her as he turned to leave. "Later, darlin'."

She watched Legend walk up the dock and turned her attention to Tyler, who tucked his gun into the back of his jeans and crouched at the end of the pier. "You set off the perimeter alarm with your little impromptu skinny-dip."

"I did?"

"Yeah, you did. You should have stayed in the house."

"You should have told me I was supposed to." She couldn't believe they were actually having this conversation. She was naked in the lake, only a few feet away from him!

He glared at her a few minutes, then shrugged. "You're right. I forgot to mention that. We'll go through all that today. In the meantime, you should get out of there."

"I was just about to. Turn around." She swam around the side near the stairs and waited. He didn't budge.

"Tyler. Turn around."

He shook his head, his eyes glued to her every move. "I'm guarding you. I have to watch to make sure you don't take a stray bullet as you get out of the water."

She rolled her eyes. "That's ridiculous. I'm all puckery now and I need to get out."

"Puckery, huh? I'd like to see that." He made no move to turn, stand or in any way avert his riveted attention.

"Are you twelve years old? Turn around!"

"Nope."

He was clearly enjoying this. "Fine, then. If you don't

turn around I'll just step out of the water naked."

He stood and crossed his arms. "Don't let me stop you."

The water that had once cooled her body boiled around her heated skin. Normally she'd never parade around naked in front of a near stranger, especially a co-worker. But damn if he didn't just irritate her enough to do just that.

He probably thought she didn't have the guts to do it.

He was wrong.

She reached for the handle on the ladder and slowly climbed up, feeling his gaze burn every inch of skin she revealed. For some reason, that made her ascend much more slowly than she normally would have.

He turned her on, no doubt about that. She wanted to do the same to him. Judging from the growing bulge in his jeans, she'd succeeded.

Determined to stand her ground, she drew her hand through her hair to wring out the excess water. "How about my shirt?"

His eyes were dark. Dangerous. Filled with a promise she knew damn well he didn't intend to keep. "This shirt?"

Yes, that one. The one dangling from his fingers like a rabbit-enticing carrot.

"Would it go with these?" He twirled the panties around in his other hand, right before he slipped them in his pocket.

"Yes, those too. Do you mind?"

"Seeing you naked? Hell no, I don't mind."

"Well Legend might. Unless you don't care if I parade down the walk and back to the house this way."

"Honey, I doubt Legend would mind one bit," he replied with a smirk. But he handed her the shirt and panties.

She tossed the shirt over her head and left the panties dangling from her fingers. "I'll go get dressed."

The shirt covered her ass...barely, but she felt his gaze on her as she walked back up to the house, her body on fire from the heated looks he gave her. His eyes had caressed her body as if he touched her and she felt every single inch of her body go up in flames.

Once she was out of eyesight she scurried into the house.

She had nothing to wear except the clothes she'd arrived in last night. Despite the fact they needed laundering, she slipped them on and raked her fingers through her tangled hair. When she came out, Tyler was alone in the kitchen.

"Where's Legend?"

"He left. Why?"

"No reason, just wondering." She reached around him to grab a glass from the cabinet and turned on the tap. "By the way, you have nothing edible in this house and I'm starving. Any chance of buying some real food?"

He leaned against the counter. "Yeah, I can do that. I had a meeting this morning and was going to stop at the store, but the beeper went off and I had to race back here. What kind of food would you like?"

"Why can't I go with you?"

He shook his head. "Bad idea. We don't know who's watching."

"Surely we're safe out here."

"Many dead people thought they were safe."

He was deliberately trying to frighten her, but she had enough common sense to know the only place she wasn't safe was her home. "I want to go with you."

"No."

"Fine," she said, gritting her teeth. "Here's my list. First, I need shampoo and conditioner, but I like the ones with the vanilla scent. Then I need a toothbrush and toothpaste. I don't like the ones that curve and the bristles have to be extra soft. As far as toothpaste, I like the mint flavored, but in gel, not paste. And get the kind with mouthwash in it. Next are tampons—"

He blanched and his eyes widened. "You can go with me."

She figured as much.

"I need clothes, too. Unless you're willing to stop by my apartment and let me pick up a few things."

"Absolutely not."

"Then I guess you'll have to whisk me by the mall."

"You're joking."

She suppressed a laugh at the man-horrified-by-shopping look on his face. "I never joke about shopping. But I promise to be quick about it. I need a few days' worth of things to wear. Surely this whole imprisonment thing won't last too long."

"It could last a lot longer."

She pulled out a kitchen chair. "How much longer?"

"Indefinitely."

That wasn't what she needed to hear right now. "I need money, Tyler. I have bills to pay. I have to work."

"You *are* working. Or you will be. You're in training right now, remember? So don't worry about money. You're still on the payroll. But right now, you can't go to work, you can't go home. We've been over this once already and until this mess is cleaned up, you need protection."

She glared at him, insulted that he would think her incompetent. "I don't need a babysitter. I can take care of myself."

"Yeah, right," he snorted. "You did a great job of that last night."

"I think we've already established my screw up of last night. Unless you have something new to add, I'd appreciate if we could drop that particular subject." She was tired of being blamed for this debacle.

Tyler shrugged, pushed away from the counter and stood in front of the table. "Let's get this shopping ordeal out of the way. After that we'll worry about the next step."

Irritated and not really knowing why, she rose and followed him out the door.

Next step. Yes, he controlled everything, didn't he? She already knew the next step. He was dumping her as soon as he could, training or no training. It was clear he didn't want her around. And while she knew it was purely a business decision, she took it personally.

Which was stupid. Agents didn't take things personally. Work was impersonal. Tyler was impersonal.

Besides, it wasn't like Tyler was her lover and had just informed her he no longer wanted anything to do with her. He was an agent and doing his job. He was her fantasy, not her reality. Reality had nothing to do with getting involved in a relationship with an agent who risked his life on a daily basis, despite how her body reacted to him.

No way. When she found someone to settle down with, it would be a man who had a routine, boring job, someone she could count on to still be alive at the end of the day. Which sure as hell didn't fit the description of an NCA field agent.

That kind of romance didn't fit into her carefully controlled life at all. The sooner she got away from Tyler, the better. She'd only loved two people in her life—her parents. They were both dead and she hadn't been able to do a thing to control that. No, loving a man whose life hung in the balance every day was not in the cards for her. It was just too painful.

So why did the thought of never seeing him again bring back that all-too-familiar feeling of loss?

Some questions were better left unanswered. Questioning her feelings for Tyler Call was one of them.

Chapter Four

ಐ

Nevada felt much better now that the pantry and refrigerator were stocked with food and she had something else to wear besides her work clothes and Tyler's T-shirt. In fact, considering she didn't have a dime to her name at the moment, he had been very generous.

Outfitted in a pair of turquoise surf shorts and a plain white tank top, Nevada was finally comfortable. Now she wasn't overdressed or underdressed, the latter having made her the most nervous, especially with the way Tyler looked at her.

After the clothing trip, they'd stopped at a grocery store and bought enough food to last a week. Nevada resisted the urge to tear into the fresh fruit while they pushed the cart up the aisles, but she was nearly starving. By the time they reached the house, she literally pushed Tyler out of the way so she could get to the food.

Having polished off the best peanut butter and jelly sandwich she'd ever had, washed down with a huge glass of milk, she was finally satiated.

Tyler had unpacked the groceries while she ate, giving her a chance to look at him without having to do it out of the corner of her eye.

He was magnificent. It was sinful the way a pair of blue jeans fit him. They were dark, tight but not too tight and wrapped around a finely sculpted ass that had her itching to reach out and touch him. His biceps hardened as he lifted the bags of groceries onto the counter. He must work out. Beautifully shaped muscles like that didn't occur without a little effort.

She sighed, whether from the delicious lunch or the specimen of sexy man before her, she wasn't certain.

Tyler turned to her. "Feeling better?"

"Much. I was hungrier than I thought."

He smiled and turned her world upside down. His straight, white teeth and perfect mouth made her yearn to have a small slice of Tyler for dessert.

"I was afraid you were going to gnaw through the baloney package before we even reached the checkout line."

She laughed not embarrassed at all. "It was touch-and-go there for awhile but I resisted."

"I'm glad you did. I'd hate to make Handi-Mart Grocery's Ten Most Wanted list. Although it would be a unique experience. I've never been on the run with a gorgeous and ravenous brunette."

Gorgeous? Surely she hadn't heard right. She brushed it off, certain he'd said something else entirely. "Umm, so what's next?"

He shrugged. "I need to do some work on the computer. We'll have dinner later."

She nodded, already salivating at the thought of dinner. "That sounds fine. Is there anything I can do to help you?"

"With what?"

"Your work."

One brow arched. "No thanks." He walked out of the room.

She'd seen that look on his face. He thought she was an idiot. That you-couldn't-possibly-do-my-job kind of smug, condescending look. She could very well do his job and had been promoted to do just that.

So he'd left her in the kitchen to do what? The cooking?

Ha! If he thought he could go off and play secret agent while she stayed here and did all the domestic stuff, he was full of shit. This wasn't the fifties when women stayed home and took care of the house and the men went to work.

Armed with a romance novel she'd picked up at the store, she marched into the living room and plopped on the couch, put her feet up and opened the latest and greatest. A little escapism and fantasy was just what she needed to keep her mind off Mr.-High-and-Mighty-Secret-Agent, Tyler Call.

Fortunately, the book was good and she found herself absorbed completely, until she heard him clear his throat. She peered over the top of the book at him. "Did you want something?"

"I'm kind of hungry," he said, his face hidden by the computer monitor.

"And?"

"How about dinner?"

"Sounds like a great idea," she replied, keeping her face firmly planted in her book. He wasn't seriously suggesting she do the cooking, was he?

"Are you ready to eat?"

"Yep."

"Let's go cook, then."

Okay, he surprised her. He fiddled with something on the computer and then rose, heading into the kitchen. She heard the sound of pots and pans being removed from the cabinet. Maybe she'd just sit there and let *him* cook *her* dinner!

"How about a couple steaks, salad and a baked potato?" he hollered from the kitchen.

Her stomach grumbled. Again. "Sounds good."

She went back to her book, but read the same paragraph

over and over again. The sounds of Tyler working in the kitchen broke her concentration.

Maybe she'd just go in there and watch him.

She strolled in with her empty glass, intending to grab a refill of iced tea. He was washing lettuce and slicing tomatoes. The guilt mixed in her stomach along with the hunger. "What can I do to help?"

"You could shred the carrots and slice the mushrooms." He held out a fat mushroom. "Do you like them in your salad?"

Nodding, she took it from his hands. She washed and sliced the vegetables while he prepared the steak and started the grill.

They worked together in companionable silence. "Amazing. You actually know how to cook," she stated as they set the table together.

He grinned. "Do you think I eat takeout all the time?"

He had a point there. "I guess not. Most single men I know don't cook."

"Their loss. I'm not an out-of-the-box-into-the-microwave kind of eater. I like my food fresh. So, I had to learn to cook."

The steaks finally ready, they sat at the table and ate.

"Who taught you to cook?" she asked, surprised at the flavor of the steak. He'd done more to it than just toss it on the grill. It had a sharp, tangy flavor that no barbecue sauce could duplicate.

"My mom."

She ignored the painful pang. "Good for her. Many mothers think only daughters should learn."

"Not my mother. Dad disagreed, of course; he's pretty old-fashioned about those kinds of things. But Mom said she wasn't going to send her son out in the world unprepared."

She laughed and immediately liked Tyler's mother. "She didn't want to let loose another helpless man that a woman would have to take care of?"

"I guess not." He poured wine for them both and sipped his, watching her over the rim of his glass. "And you? What about your parents?"

The easy smile on her face faded. "They're both dead."

His eyebrows rose. "I'm sorry. What happened?"

She pushed the plate away, no longer hungry. "My mother died of cancer when I was sixteen."

"Again, I'm sorry. And your father?"

"After my mom died he started drinking. Hard and every day. He lost his job because he couldn't get up and go to work, and a year later it finally killed him." And she couldn't do a damn thing to stop him. He hadn't wanted to live for *her*.

She looked up, realizing she'd just told Tyler what she'd never told anyone else. He stared at her and didn't speak. Shit, what was she thinking? She never shared her feelings like that. Not even with Ellen.

Embarrassed, she looked down, her eyes riveted on her plate until she felt his hand slide over the top of hers.

"I'm sorry, Nevada. That must have been very hard for you."

She pushed back the tears that threatened to spill. She was not going to be weak about this. "It was, but I got over it."

"What happened after that?"

"I was almost eighteen when my dad died so I was able to live by myself. I went to college on a full scholarship, got hired on afterward at the NCA and I've been there ever since."

"And that's all?"

Her eyes swept up at his question, searching his face. She almost laughed at his wide-eyed expression. "Yes, that's all. Should there be more?"

He shrugged. "I don't know. Marriage maybe, kids, something. How about relationships? Boyfriends?"

Boy, was he nosy. "Not really. I'm not into any kind of permanent relationships."

"Why not?"

Was this an inquisition? "Because I'm not interested." Time to turn the tables. "What about you?"

"I'm too busy and travel too much to have a relationship. Some day, maybe I'll be ready to settle down, but for now my work is my love."

So he was running, just like her. She wondered what his reasons really were, then cast the thought aside.

Don't get personal. Don't care about him. That could only lead to more trouble than she was already in.

After dinner, they cleaned the dishes together. Working side by side with Tyler was relaxing. Having him near made her feel comfortable.

And uncomfortable at the same time. She watched him scrub pots and pans, amazed at his willingness to help out in the kitchen. He was like no man she'd ever known before and she found herself enjoying the moments they spent together. And, despite her internal warnings, wanting more.

She leaned against the counter, drying the dishes and watching the way his body moved, wishing things were different. Wishing *she* was different.

"Stop that."

Her gaze flew up to meet his. "Stop what?"

"Stop looking at me like that."

"Like what?"

"Like you want to eat me alive." The smile flamed in his eyes, riveting her gaze to him.

"I…I…" *Speak, you idiot.* "I did no such thing. And if I did, I didn't mean to."

He raised an eyebrow. "Didn't mean to what? Look at me like that?"

She nodded, suddenly mute and feeling stupid for thinking this way about him. She was supposed to remind herself that he was an arrogant bastard, not potential dessert.

"You can't help the way you look at me, any more than I can help the way I look at you." He stepped toward her and she began to sweat. He took the towel out of her hands and threw it on the counter, then took her hands in his. "There's a flash of heat between us. I feel it. I know you do too."

There shouldn't be, but he was right. She felt it too. A spark, like lightning, tingeing the air with electricity.

This wasn't happening. The mere touch of his hands flamed her body and it reacted like it enjoyed the burn. Her breasts swelled, her nipples pressing hard against the soft cotton of her shirt. Her pussy ached and moistened. A severe chemical reaction to one potent, testosterone-laden male.

When was the last time a man had touched her body? She'd always kept relationships to a bare minimum, never getting past the point of involvement. Sex had been quick, more for release than emotional connection. Most of the time she just did it herself, imagining the man of her fantasies doing delicious things to her body and making her scream with a climax she couldn't hold back.

Tyler had been the man she fantasized about. And now her fantasy man was right here, touching her. Despite her fear of involvement, she wanted to step into his arms and take the chance of being hurt, just to feel alive.

"Do you feel it?" His voice was no more than a whispered caress over her cheek.

"Yes."

"Did you know your eyes turn a molten gold when you look at me?"

She shook her head.

He pulled her toward him, her breasts sliding against the thin cotton of his shirt. She gasped at the contact of his hard chest against the softness of her breasts.

"This is dangerous," he said, his voice thick and heavy with sensual promise.

"Dangerous?"

He nodded and trailed his fingers along her cheek. She leaned into his hand, welcoming his touch. "Very dangerous. Like your eyes, pulling me in. Hypnotizing me. I shouldn't want…"

As his words trailed off, she closed her eyes, captured by his voice. It resonated through her, shaking her resolve, eradicating her fear. She inhaled a shaky breath, but knew all hope was lost if he kissed her.

"What is it you don't want?" she asked, captured by his touch. He slid his fingers over her lips—slow, soft, agonizingly gentle.

"This." The first touch of his lips against hers was lightning, searing her with a shock of instant desire. He pressed his mouth firmly against hers and she exploded.

She burned, roasting alive in the exquisite fire of his kiss. He tasted of wine and passion and she wanted to drink him in. He reached for her, threading his fingers through her hair and pulling her ever closer to his scorching heat.

His body was hard, his erection rocking insistently

against the juncture of her thighs. Instinctively she moved against him and he groaned into her mouth.

"And this," he said as he pulled his mouth away from hers and pressed fevered kisses to the side of her neck. She shivered, barely able to keep her knees from buckling. His hands on the bare flesh of her arms and shoulders heated her blood to boiling.

She shouldn't want this. It was wrong, risky, made her feel out of control in ways she'd never felt before. But she didn't want it to stop.

"I don't want to want you, Nevada, but I do." He dragged his lips from hers, his eyes smoldering with a barely contained fire.

The abrupt change in his demeanor confused her. First, he was hot and passionate, then he backed away as if she'd burned him.

Her lips still trembled from his kiss, her body quaking with the need for completion. How could he just stop?

"We can't do this. I have a mission, a job to do. Having an affair with you doesn't fit into my plans."

He might as well have slapped her, the shock to her system so painful it roared through her like an aching flu. First he told her he wanted her, now he didn't want her, yet he'd kissed her with the longing of a man who'd lived alone on a deserted island for the past ten years.

She wiped her lips with the back of her hand, trying to send as painful a message to him as the one she'd just received. "Who said you'd get one? An affair isn't something I want either. I have an easy solution for you, Tyler," she said as she quickly covered the hurt with the control she'd mastered over the years. "Don't touch me like that again, don't kiss me and you'll get over it soon enough."

"That simple, is it?" He crossed his arms in front of his

chest, closing her off. He'd withdrawn completely from her, the open warmth in his eyes now safely shielded by a steel curtain.

"Yes, it's that simple." She'd effectively masked her attraction to him before, when he was nothing more than a voice. Detached, unreal, perfect in her fantasies, which is exactly where she was going to put Tyler Call. Back where he belonged. "It's easy enough for me to do, surely you can do it too."

"Fine," he said, his voice laced with resignation. "That's just fine." Without another glance in her direction, he walked out of the room.

Nevada sighed, trying desperately to get her shaky emotions under control. He'd started this, with that kiss and those fiery looks. And now he thought he could control the situation by shutting off his emotions. Well, two could play that game, and in the game of control and burying her emotions deep, she was the master.

* * * * *

Tyler busied himself at the boat dock, scrubbing down the deck that didn't really need to be cleaned. But he needed to work off some energy from his encounter with Nevada.

What had he been thinking? He knew better than to touch her, but she tantalized him in those barely-covering-her-thighs shorts and skimpy little shirt. Then, to top it off, she gave him that look that clearly indicated she wanted him. More than wanted him. More like she wanted to devour him. He hadn't misread the hunger in her eyes knew his own mirrored what she felt.

Instead of walking away like he should, he'd pulled her into his arms and taken what she willingly offered. And it shattered his carefully controlled world to pieces. She tasted like sweet vanilla and at that moment he'd never wanted anyone more than he wanted Nevada.

But, he didn't want to want her. He couldn't want her. The mission was paramount, within his grasp. Yet he trailed after her like a lovesick teenager. In the meantime, the mission was taking a back burner when it should be front and center.

His father would be appalled if he could see him now. He remembered the pride on his parents' faces when he'd graduated from military school and then followed his father's example with his entry into the NCA. He'd never be a hero like his dad, but he'd damn sure follow the rules the same way.

The first thing he'd have to do is focus on his job. The second and harder thing would be to ignore the woman living in his house.

He attacked the deck with a new zest, confident he had his desire for Nevada under control. And when it came to control, Tyler was the master.

Chapter Five

Tyler was ignoring her. Sitting over at the desk, hiding behind the computer monitor with keys clicking away, not paying the slightest bit of attention to her. Not that it mattered — she was ignoring him, too.

Nevada had almost finished the novel she'd started earlier. Now she was riveted at the climactic moment. Would Charles arrive at the fog-laden dock in time to save Jacquelin, the love of his life? Or would the stalker find her first? She hurriedly flipped the page to find out.

"What are you doing over there?"

She looked up from the book. *He speaks.* "I'm reading."

"What's that god-awful sound?"

"Pardon me?"

"There's a really annoying sound coming from your location. Are you biting your nails?"

She quickly spit out the remnants of a former fingernail. "Of course not." Damn.

He made no further comments so she returned to her book. She couldn't turn the pages fast enough. The action boiled, ready to erupt. They were just about to find out who the stalker was.

"Dammit all to hell!"

She jumped at Tyler's loud curse and dropped the book in her lap. "What's wrong?"

"Nothing."

He sounded like a pouting little kid. "Obviously there's

something. What is it?"

Instead of spitting it out, he produced a series of low mumbles. The only words she'd managed to understand were *damn computer* and *pain in the ass*. Since the ass in question wasn't sitting on the monitor, he must be having a problem with the computer.

"What's wrong with the computer?" Unable to ignore him any longer, she walked over to the desk and leaned over the monitor.

He looked up at her with frustrated eyes, brows furrowed and lines crossing his forehead. "The Internet sucks."

She fought back the smile that threatened to erupt. "That's a pretty broad statement. Care to narrow it down?"

"No."

It was easy to figure out his problem. "You're having trouble with a search. What are you looking for?" She walked around the desk and stood next to him, peering at the information on the screen.

"I know what I want to find, I just can't find it."

"I understand. Same thing happens to me all the time. Let me do it."

He squinted at her and she felt like she was being inspected. Was he trying to decide if she could be trusted with his secret information? What a moron! She should walk back to her book and let him figure his problem out alone.

Trying unsuccessfully to hide her growing irritation, she lifted her chin and crossed her arms. "I'm not a spy, you know. Might I remind you we work for the same company?"

"Actually, I was admiring your...what do women call those things?" He tilted his head toward her baby blue boxers and tank top.

"I call them pajamas."

"Oh. Whatever. They're nice."

Nice? That meant he hated them. She understood men's lingo. Hot is great. Sexy is perfect. Nice is boring. She didn't want to be nice. She wanted to be hot and sexy.

After a couple roving glances over her body, his gaze fixated on her face. Finally, she grew uncomfortable with his scrutiny and wiped her mouth, just in case some stray fingernail remnants remained. "Do you want me to help you or not?" She prayed he did. Anything to keep him from staring at her.

He shrugged. "I guess so. Sit down." They switched places and he leaned over her. She inhaled his crisp scent, felt his heat despite the inches that separated them. This was even worse than the staring.

"First off," she said as she got her bearings, "whatever you're looking for isn't going to be found using this search engine. Since I assume it's about the case, I'm switching to one more user-friendly and information savvy." She quickly punched in a website address which brought up her favorite search engine. "I use this one all the time at the agency. What are you looking for?"

"The trucking company that owned the semi I took a ride underneath."

"Okay. That should be easy enough. What have you looked at so far?"

"Publicly traded companies. It isn't one."

"I could have told you that." If he'd have bothered to ask for her help when he started. Stubborn man.

She pulled up some of the federal databases that listed information on privately held trucking companies. "What do you have on it?"

"License tag, but useless. It was bogus and most likely stolen or dummied. I did get a company name off the truck cab, but can't find any information on it."

"What's the name?"

"Cross Country Trucking."

After typing in the name of the company, she sat back and waited for the search engine to do its job.

Waiting had its drawbacks. He laid his hand against the back of her chair, the hairs of his forearm tickling the back of her neck. With his hip resting against her shoulder, she was at eye level with his…

"Now *there's* something."

Indeed it was. But he meant on the monitor. She turned to review the details. Tyler did too, bending forward and leaning against her as he scanned the screen. His arm brushed hers. She hoped the computer was grounded because a spark of electricity lit up her insides when their skin touched. "Would you like to pull up a chair?"

"No, thanks. I can see fine here."

Great.

"So what does all this mean?"

"It's kind of tricky, but I've seen it before. A dummy corporation, here," she said as she pointed to the company's official name. "Some privately held companies don't want anyone to know who really owns them, so they set up through multiple channels. But," she added as she typed in a series of codes into the search database, "we're smarter than they are."

She waited for what she knew would appear. "*Voilà*. The owners."

Tyler's eyes widened. "I'll be damned."

Nevada tried not to beam, but it sure felt good to do something useful for a change. And to show him she wasn't a complete idiot. Which, of course, he should have known already had he bothered to pull his head out of his ass.

"How did you do that?"

She would not smile smugly. Really, she wouldn't. All right, maybe a little. "That's what the agency pays me to do. That's what I'm good at."

"I'll say." He reached behind her to turn on the printer, his chest brushing her back. Her skin tingled and her errant nipples hardened. How did he manage to do that to her?

"You want me to hit the print button?"

He nodded and walked over to the printer, pulling the pages off as quickly as they were through. "Wow," he said, rapidly scanning the information. "You're good."

Nevada may not know Tyler all that well, but she knew him well enough to realize he didn't throw out compliments easily. "Thanks."

He took the printout to the couch and sat, propping his feet on the coffee table in front of him. So now what was she supposed to do? Sit here, or go back and retrieve her book? Then what? Move to the chair so she wouldn't have to sit next to him? Why was something so simple suddenly so complicated?

She couldn't very well go to bed. He was sitting on it. Which of course got her mind racing with visions of leaping on top of him and having her way with him. She squeezed her legs together to massage the incessant ache between them, wishing he would leave so she could indulge her fantasies with a little hand work.

"Come over here. I could use your help."

Yeah, she could use a hand herself, she thought with a smile. But at least his request solved her immediate problem. She headed toward him, hesitating between the couch and the chair. After a couple seconds of mental debate, she chose the chair and sat, waiting for his question.

Tyler looked up and frowned. "Not there. Here." He patted the empty spot next to him on the small couch.

"I don't want to crowd you." God, she was such a coward. She risked her life to save him at the warehouse. Now she acted petrified at the thought of sitting near him. What was wrong with her?

"Don't be stupid. I need you to help me with this information and I want to point and talk at the same time. I won't bite."

His grin was disconcerting. Reluctantly she left the safe haven of the chair and sat next to him on the couch.

"Unless you ask me to."

Her gaze flew to his. Dark amusement danced in the depths and a devilish smile lit up his face. "You look like you just walked out in the middle of a gruesome horror movie. What is it? Do I smell?"

Yes, you do. Like sex and every forbidden thing I ever wanted. "No, you don't. What can I help you with?"

"Look here." He pointed to a list of names and addresses. "These are the owners, right?"

She nodded and scanned the list. "Typically, a privately held company will set up a dummy corporation to hide the true owners. No laws prevent them from doing so. International and American mixed companies sometimes form a merged company. They're listed as the owners, which is what you see here."

"Which means Mercado International is the primary owner of the trucking company?"

"Right."

"Can you find out who the owners of Mercado International are?"

She nodded. "Yes. It'll take some time, but I can do it."

"Good. You can get started on it in the morning."

Their eyes met. His thigh touched hers. She felt feverish, sweaty and moist in places that had no business moistening. She had to get a grip on her libido. *Come on, Nevada. Where's that famous control you're always spouting off about? Now would be a good time to use it.*

She cleared her throat. "You're welcome." She started to get up but he grabbed her arm.

"Wait."

Oh God, please don't make me stay here, sitting next to you, soaking in the depths of your eyes, breathing in your scent, making me want...

What did she want? "Yes?"

They were so close she could almost count the number of long, curling lashes surrounding his dark eyes. He'd moved his arm behind her neck, his hand playing with the trailing wisps of hair that had come loose from her high ponytail. She shivered.

He smiled. "Cold?"

"Nuh-uh." Now, there was a coherent response. *Brilliant, Nevada.*

He massaged the muscles in the back of her neck. She couldn't help it; she rested her head on the palm of his hand and let him work his magic. She closed her eyes and imagined his touch on other aching parts of body.

"Do you like that?"

"Yes." What wasn't there to like? His fingers sent a rush of sensation throughout her body faster than the blood flowing through her veins. Her bodily fluids went into overdrive in preparation for something she couldn't deny she wanted and her heart accelerated to racing speed.

"Good."

With her eyes closed, it was just like she used to imagine him. His voice was low and husky, whispering in her ear, calling to her desire, her needs.

"I want to kiss you again, Nevada."

Then kiss me, dammit! Make love to me. Do what neither of us should do but both of us want. "You do?"

"Yes, I do."

She smiled at his answer. "Well, then, now what?"

He continued to rub her neck. She couldn't open her eyes, afraid of what she'd see reflected in his.

Finally, she heard him sigh and remove his hands. "It's late. Let's get some sleep."

Sleep? Sleep? Was he kidding? Her eyes flew open in shock and her mind screamed, *Fuck me, you idiot!* He was already halfway to the bedroom. He paused at the doorway and stared back at her with a mixture of regret and heat.

"Night, Nevada."

She couldn't form a coherent word to save her life, so she simply nodded. He pivoted and went to bed.

He'd touched her, sent magical impulses through her brain and body. He'd told her he wanted to kiss her. And then he left and went to bed. What was she supposed to make of all that?

Frankly, she was getting tired of this teasing cat and mouse game he played with her. He either wanted her or he didn't.

She plopped her head on the pillow of the couch and grabbed her book. She gave up. Men. She'd never understand the way their minds worked.

Maybe Charles would have better luck with Jacqueline. After all, he was a fantasy man, just like Tyler used to be. Only in her fantasy world would the man she desired make all her dreams come true.

Except her mind refused to concentrate on the characters in her book. Her body was still inflamed by Tyler's touch, her lips still feeling his mouth on her, his tongue coaxing its way inside and tasting her.

Her nipples beaded under her top. Reaching up, she shut off the light, keeping her eyes glued to the door of his bedroom. His lights were off, telling her he'd gone to sleep.

Obviously he hadn't been as worked up as she was. Or maybe he was contemplating doing the same thing she was about to do.

Quick, easy, just to take the edge off. God knows Tyler had been tantalizing her to the brink anyway. This wouldn't take long.

She reached under the hem of her shirt and lifted it, exposing her breasts to the night air. Her nipples rose and pebbled, aching for Tyler's mouth. Instead, she slid her palms back and forth over the distended buds, feeling them swell and harden more. She rolled the nipples between her thumb and forefinger, plucking them into sharp peaks, the sensation shooting between her legs.

Which was exactly where she wanted her hands. She trailed her fingertips lightly over her ribs and belly, then slipped them underneath the waistband of her boxers, searching and finding the heat of her sex. With a quiet sigh she found her clit and lightly caressed it. Dewy moisture slickened her sex as she moved one hand down over her slit, then quickly thrust two fingers inside her pussy, lifting her buttocks from the couch as she fucked herself with one hand and rubbed her clit with the other.

She'd give anything to have one of her vibrators right now, something long and hard to slip inside her cunt and fuck herself to a blinding orgasm.

But she didn't. And she didn't have Tyler's cock inside her, which was what she'd really wanted. So she'd settle for imagining him opening his bedroom door and walking toward her, his naked body visible in the moonlight streaming through the windows. His cock was hard, ready, as he stroked it with his hand while he approached.

Her legs parted and she petted her clit, keeping her gaze trained on him as he climbed above her, settled between her legs and drove home with one, quick thrust. He took her mouth at the same time, silencing her cries of pleasure as he stroked her, harder, faster, like a wild rollercoaster that dipped and careened around the corners so fast she couldn't catch a breath.

Nevada bit down on her bottom lip to keep from crying out as the waves of her climax crashed over her. Her pussy squeezed her fingers as the intense orgasm milked them, just as if her fingers were Tyler's shaft.

She panted through the remnants of pleasure pulses, withdrew her fingers and righted her clothing, wishing for all the world that her fantasies had become a reality tonight.

Satiated, temporarily at least, she prayed for at least a few hours' sleep.

* * * * *

Tyler tossed and turned in bed, glaring at the clock that signaled he'd been trying to sleep for the better part of two hours. *Idiot. Moron. Dumbass.* How could he continually make the same mistakes over and over again?

Why did he tell her he wanted to kiss her? Where was his so called master control? Yeah, right. That was a laugh. He pulled his hands through his hair, his body heated to boiling, his hard-on refusing to go away.

It was his own damn fault that he had been erect for several hours, his cock refusing to let him sleep.

First, he had to lean over Nevada at the computer, smell her freshly washed hair, that scent of vanilla that lingered even after she left a room. Then, he had to touch her, rub her neck, feel the soft cotton of her pajamas and the heat of her skin through the material. Her skin. Like warmed silk. He ached so bad to touch her again he almost groaned out loud.

Her hair had been draped silk over his arm as she'd rested her head on his hand; he could feel the tension in her muscles melt under his fingers. He wanted to ease that tension for both of them—that never ending feeling of wanting so badly it was almost painful.

But that wasn't going to do either of them good in this situation. They were temporarily forced into close proximity and both healthy adults. Of course they'd get the hots for each other. Well, hell. Who wouldn't have the hots for Nevada, with her exotic looks and long legs?

That didn't mean he needed to do anything about it.

Master of control, his ass. He was going to have to do better.

How could he control anything when he couldn't even beat his unruly cock into behaving itself?

Blowing out a frustrated breath, he reached down and firmly grasped the offending member in hand, bound and determined to squeeze the life out of it. Or at least a good come, so that maybe, just maybe, he could get a little sleep tonight.

The shaft was hot, pulsing, his balls tight and ready for release. This wouldn't take long. He'd been primed for a fuck since early tonight and, if he wasn't so damn stupid, he could have sunk inside Nevada several hours ago. The way she responded told him she'd felt the same way.

But a sound outside his bedroom made him pause mid-stroke. It started out almost a whisper, but then grew until it reached a crescendo. Tyler sat up and listened. It was Nevada and she was crying.

He pulled the covers back and reached for his boxers on the floor before hurrying into the living room.

"No, please. Please don't leave me. Daddy, no! Don't go!"

Flipping the light switch in the bedroom illuminated the couch enough for him to see her. The light coverlet was clenched tight in her fists, her face scrunched up as if she were in pain. Tyler sat on the edge of the couch and gently touched her shoulders.

"Nevada, wake up."

"No, Daddy no! Don't go! Not like Mommy! Please Daddy, don't you leave me too! I need you!"

Her sobs tore at his heart. Her face was wet from the tears flowing down her cheeks.

Tyler clutched her shoulders firmly and shook her. "Nevada. Wake up!"

Her eyes opened wide as she bolted upright on the couch. Focusing on Tyler's face, she threw her arms around his neck, pressing her tear-stained cheek against his throat. Without a word she held onto him, the sobs racking her body until she shook uncontrollably.

He wrapped one arm around her shoulders and the other under her legs, pulling her onto his lap. Leaning against the back of the couch, he cradled her in his arms, holding her as tight as he dared. She pressed closer, seemingly unable to stop the flow of tears caused by her nightmare.

Having no concept of what to do for her, he held her, rocked her as he would a child and stroked her hair, whispering softly that everything would be all right. His throat tightened as he felt her misery flow outward. What she must have suffered losing her parents. Had she held all this pain inside all these years?

"It's okay, baby, shh, everything will be fine." At this

moment, this one moment, time stood still. Tyler's heart swelled with tenderness, an unfamiliar feeling. He wanted to take her pain away more than he had ever wanted anything before.

Nevada finally calmed down, the sobs reduced to sniffles and hiccups. He leaned them both forward and grabbed the box of tissues from the coffee table, handing her a few that she accepted with a choked thanks. But she made no attempt to move from his lap and he wasn't about to let her go.

Her head rested on his chest, the rise and fall of his breathing bringing the top of her head up to his nose. With every inhale, he took in her sweet scent, and managed to grasp a little more tightly to her. If he wasn't careful, she was going to make him cry. He almost laughed out loud at the thought. Big, tough agent reduced to tears by woman's nightmares. Dylan would love that one.

Finally, she stirred, placing her hand on his chest, giving herself a slight push to prop up her head.

Tyler stopped breathing. Her eyes were luminous wet gold from her tears. They shone with a brightness he thought was a dream. She managed a tremulous smile, and tore him apart.

"Thank you," she sniffed. "God, I'm so embarrassed."

"For what?"

"For waking you. I had a nightmare. I'm really not a crybaby. Geez, this is mortifying."

He continued to stroke her silken hair. "Nothing wrong with crying over a bad dream. Was it about your father?"

"Yes."

"Do you want to talk about it? It might help." He swept a leftover tear from her cheek. She leaned into his hand. God. Like a magnet. He cupped her chin and pressed a light kiss to her lips.

"It's stupid. Nothing, really."

"Nightmares are never stupid. Tell me about it."

She tilted her head to the side and studied him as if she couldn't quite believe he was real. Admittedly, this tenderness he felt toward her was a foreign concept to him, too.

"It was about the night my father died. He'd been in a drunken stupor for days and as usual I couldn't do anything to help him. He didn't want my help. He wanted to die and I couldn't do a thing to stop him."

"Why do you think he wanted to die?"

"Because my mother died and she was his entire life."

"That can't be true. He had you."

"I wasn't enough for him to live for." Her eyelashes swept down over her cheeks as she looked away, fresh tears dropping onto his hand.

He tilted her chin up and forced her to meet his eyes. "You *are* worth living for."

She shrugged. "It doesn't matter. I know how much he loved my mother. When she died, he died too. It just took him a little longer."

"Nevada, it's not your fault."

"I know. I tried to control it, but I couldn't keep it from happening."

He leaned back. "You think you can control how people feel? You have no power over the things people do. You can give them your opinion, tell them how you feel, but in the end it's their choice." He saw that often enough in his work. Everyone had a choice. Some made the right ones and unfortunately, a lot of them made the wrong ones.

She touched his cheek. "You make it sound so simple."

He laughed lightly. "Simple? Not really."

"Well, anyway," she said, her voice as soft as the pajamas she wore, "thank you."

"You're welcome."

"I suppose we should try to get some sleep now?"

He looked at her, her eyes wide with the pain she tried so hard to hide. And something else. Something he knew he'd see in his own reflection. A desperate longing, a desire to belong to someone. To hold someone.

Goddamit! He didn't want to have these feelings. But he'd held back long enough.

"Not yet," he replied, pulling her against his chest and capturing her mouth in a searing kiss.

Chapter Six

ॐ

Tyler's warm lips melted into hers, stealing her breath away. Nevada tasted the salt of her own tears, making the kiss even more bittersweet.

She wanted to tell him so many things, but her mind wouldn't concentrate on forcing her voice to work. All she could manage were mumbles and moans of pleasure as his hands caressed her back, splaying against her heated skin.

It meant so much to have him wake her from the torment of the past. How comforting it had been to be held in his arms as she cried out her grief for the parents she missed so desperately.

But now, all she could focus on was how it felt to be in his arms. She grasped his corded biceps, the muscles bunching as he shifted her down against the couch. He had such strength, power that could easily snap her in two. Yet was so gentle as his body covered hers, holding his weight off her with little effort.

Tyler's midnight eyes burned into her as his hands spoke what words could never say. His arousal pressed against her hip, his tight, determined expression providing no apology for his desire.

Her body cried out for him, wanting him in ways she'd never wanted another man. Wholly, completely, she craved a merging she'd backed away from before.

With any other man in her past, it had just been sex. With Tyler, it was so much more. It both frightened and thrilled her at the same time.

"Touch me, Nevada," he whispered with a desperate sense of urgency. She did, sliding her hands up his arms to clench his shoulders, then down his chest, winding her fingers through the sprinkling of dark, curling hair.

Her palms circled his nipples, gliding lightly against the hardening nubs. He groaned and she delighted in her power. Desperate to feel the length of him pressed against her, she grasped the back of his neck and pulled his mouth against hers. When their lips made contact, she raised her hips until her sex met the raging steel of his cock. The voltage level of desire shot higher.

He moved and her body wept its desire.

"You know I love these pajama things," he said, his voice dark as the moonless night, "but they're in my way." He swept the tank top up and over her stomach, then eased his way down to press his lips against her bare flesh.

She gasped as he lifted the shirt over her breasts, sliding his hands along with it and grazing her nipples with the palms of his hands. The ache pulsed within her and she lifted her hips once again, rocking against his hardened body.

"If you don't stop that," he rasped, "my foreplay technique is going to be very brief."

"I don't need foreplay." She moved against him again, communicating the urgency of her need.

He entranced her with the ferocity of his gaze as he pulled her arms over her head and swept her top off with one swift move. His eyes shimmered in the darkness, a glimpse of moonlight through the cloudy haze. She watched in complete fascination as he covered her nipple with his lips.

"Tyler," she moaned, threading her hands through his hair. She pulled him closer until his mouth completely covered her. He laved her breast with his tongue, drawing a fire from within that only he could douse.

Why hadn't she felt this way with anyone else before? She was no virgin, and yet this was the first time she'd ever completely given herself over to the sensations of a man's touch.

She felt the chill over her breasts as he removed his mouth and leaned away, his face taut with desire, his eyes like glowing black coals in the semi-darkness.

"I want you, Nevada," he said sharply. "Tell me right now if you don't want this."

After all the starts and stops, she knew exactly what she wanted. Without hesitation, she reached for him. "Then take me," she answered swiftly as she brought her lips up to meet his. This was the moment that would change things between them. She should have thought about it, planned it, decided whether it was a good step or not.

But there was no time. And it felt right. At this moment, she wanted to make love with Tyler. Needed it, like she needed to fill her lungs with air. The risks be damned, the control she so desired completely forgotten. She wanted this and if she had to, she'd guard her heart very carefully.

A shrill beeping shot them both upright on the couch.

Tyler swore sharply. "The perimeter alarm!" he said in a harsh whisper. "Get dressed, now! We need to get the hell out of here!"

She didn't need to be told twice. Tyler ran into his bedroom and hurried back out, fastening his jeans and tossing a T-shirt over his head. Their almost-lovemaking moments ago already a distant memory, she grabbed shorts and a shirt and threw them on. Tyler grasped her hand, pulling her behind him.

"Should we turn out the light?" she asked.

He shook his head. "Don't want them to know we're aware they're here," he said into her ear. "Stay quiet and follow me. If anything happens to me, run down to the dock, jump in the boat and hightail it out of here—the keys are in the ignition."

She wouldn't think of that. Nothing was going to happen to him. She nodded and followed.

"Stay low," he whispered as he pulled a gun from the waistband of his jeans. He reached for a box in the computer desk and pulled out a couple clips of ammunition, sliding them into his front pocket. "We're going out the back door." He peered at the security monitor set on the floor under the desk. "They're out front. No one's breached the back yet."

They crawled on their hands and knees to the back door and Tyler opened it, just as the sound of a click in the front signaled someone had tried the knob.

"Get ready to run." He opened the back door a crack and pulled her outside.

Blood pounded in her ears. She tried to breathe normally, but already felt the dizziness of hyperventilation. She willed her body to slow down its reaction to her fear.

It was pitch-black outside, her eyes not yet accustomed to the impenetrable darkness. She relied solely on Tyler's hand to guide her. They crouched down and crept along the stepping-stones.

"What about those other security surprises you mentioned?"

"That'll buy us a minute or two. No more. Come on!"

The dock had seemed so close the other day. Now it stretched ahead of her like an insurmountable obstacle. They'd never make it in time. Whoever was coming for them was already in the house. Shadows appeared through the window of the dimly lit living room.

"Hurry!"

The tug of his hand spurred her on. She still couldn't see

a thing, but she'd run blind if she had to.

She heard a scream and a shouted curse coming from the house. A brief glance at Tyler told her one of his extra surprises must have caught the intruders unaware.

"A small electrical shock," he explained. "But it'll slow them down enough to be more cautious."

The pier was finally in sight, barely illuminated in the weak light over the dock. If they hurried, they might make it.

The sound of voices echoed behind her. Heavy footsteps pounded against the stepping-stones like rumbling thunder. Tyler whipped her around so she was in front of him, his hand on her back pushing her forward.

"Run!" he shouted.

A sound like firecrackers burst all around her as the popping of gunfire sped past her ears. Dirt and grass flew up, slapping at her legs. For once, she was grateful for the darkness that shielded them from their pursuers' bullets. Her throat was dry and she gasped for air as she commanded her feet to fly. She heard another pop, this one much closer.

Tyler returned fire. How could he run and shoot at people behind him? She didn't take the time to stop and look.

Her feet finally hit the wooden deck, the echo of their shoes slapping against the boards like a homing beacon to the men chasing them. She felt a breeze as Tyler whisked by, grabbing her hand again. The rhythmic sounds of water lapping against the side of the dock signaled they'd made it.

"Hang on," Tyler said as he swooped her up in his arms and stepped into the boat, immediately setting her down. "Get down in the bottom and stay there!"

Dammit, she wanted to help. Drive the boat or fire on the intruders, anything but lie there helpless. But she knew now wasn't the time to argue with Tyler, so she immediately went down on the cold floor and tried to still her shaking body.

They didn't have much time. Visions of television shows where the escapees get into the boat only to have the engine stall flew through her mind. She sent up a silent prayer that their luck would hold.

The engine roared to life and Tyler wasted no time throwing it into gear. Nevada was thankful the boat was pointed outward. He didn't have to back the boat out to make an escape. She heard the sharp ping against the side of the craft and cringed. A bullet had hit a part of it—which part she didn't know. She hoped it wasn't anything that made it move.

The boat roared out of the dock and away from the men chasing them. Nevada longed to sit up and see what was going on, but she waited for Tyler to give her the okay.

They sped along in the darkness. Every bump was a jolt deep in her bones, occasionally catapulting her entire body off the deck. She'd end up bruised from this, but was too thankful to be alive to complain.

Tyler shouted over the roar of the engine. "You can get up now."

She quickly scrambled from the deck and held on to the edge of the speedboat, making her way to his side. She leaned against him so he could hear her over the noise.

"Where are we going?"

"To the marina. About two miles from here."

She hung on and didn't say another word, knowing it was futile to engage in a shouting conversation. There'd be time for questions later, if they made it. No, *when* they made it.

Tyler maneuvered expertly in the darkness. She could only see the small areas of the lake, highlighted by the spotlight on the side of the boat. To her, it was a bunch of black water with occasional banks and trees. She'd have run them aground long ago if she were driving.

But Tyler must have night vision. They cut through the water without mishap and Nevada finally saw lights in the distance. The marina.

He slowed as they approached the near deserted harbor, then pulled into a vacant slip and stopped the engine, looping a thick rope around a wooden post.

"Here, hang on to these," he said as he bent down and retrieved a backpack and small briefcase from the cabinet under the steering wheel. She took them from him and looked around as he grabbed a few other items. No one in sight.

"They'll follow us, won't they?"

He nodded, his face creased with the tension they both felt. "They'll have to go by car. That'll buy us at least a half hour. We've gotta get out of here and fast."

"How are we going to do that?" It was the middle of the night, the marina restaurant was closed and there wasn't another business open that she could see. Everything was locked up tight and shut down until morning.

"I have a car not far from here. But we have to hurry."

She shivered in the cool night air, more from fear than the chill, and wrapped her arms around her waist. "A car? Where?"

"In storage at a garage."

He grabbed the bags and started walking. She quickly followed. "What happens if they come before we get to the car?"

The worried look on his face wasn't comforting. "Pray they don't."

She did just that. They headed away from the marina and up the hill toward a row of businesses. Nevada's heart lurched as she saw approaching headlights. Would it be the men who broke into his house?

"Step back into the shadows," he said, drawing his gun.

She waited, pressed against the side of one of the shops. Her heart raced and fear all but choked her. Finally she exhaled, relieved to see a bright yellow taxi pass by.

"Let's go," Tyler said, his pace quickening up the hill until they reached a single story metal building with a sign proclaiming it Mike's Garage.

He had a set of keys already in hand and unlocked the front door, quickly escorting Nevada inside. He shut the door and grabbed her hand.

"Can't risk the lights. Hold on."

Once again she was immersed in darkness, his hand her only lifeline. They crept along the interior wall of the building, Tyler in front of her, until he stopped. She heard the chirping of a vehicle's security system and the lights inside the car came on.

He motioned for her to get in. She did so without hesitation, but her patience was about to run out. She needed answers.

"You keep another vehicle in a mechanic's garage?"

He nodded as he threw the bags in the back seat.

"Why?"

"Because of what happened tonight. I like to keep my options open. One of the things you have to learn about being a field agent is to always have an escape planned out."

"How did you know this might happen?"

"I didn't. But in my line of work, anything is possible, including an attempt on my life. That's why the backup car."

"Good thinking," she said, shaking her head in wonder. He really was her movie star secret agent fantasy come to life.

"With my background, you learn to have more than one plan."

He opened a large sliding door at the back of the garage, jumped in the SUV and drove outside, then shut and locked the door behind them. He left the headlights off and slowly inched the vehicle toward the street. They sat there for a minute while he watched for cars, but the street remained deserted.

Finally, she exhaled. They left the area and headed toward a more populated section. Her hands still shook and she clasped them together to make them stop. There wasn't much she could do to calm the tremors throughout her body, though.

At least she hadn't embarrassed herself by throwing up or hyperventilating. She'd have to learn to keep her panic under control or she'd never make it as a field agent.

"Now where are we going?" They'd entered the freeway leading toward the downtown riverfront area.

"My place."

She turned to him. "Your place? I thought we'd been staying at your place?"

He offered a half smile. "Not really. That's where everyone thinks I live."

"But that's not your real home."

"Right."

"And now we're going where you *do* live?"

"Right again."

"Won't they find us there, too?" That's what bothered her most of all. How did they find them in the first place? And who were *they*?

"No, they won't find us there."

That's what he said before. "How can you be sure?"

"Because no one knows where it is."

"No one?"

"No one." They approached a red light and Tyler turned his gaze on her, his eyes gentling as his lips curved in a wry smile. "Well, now *you* know."

So, he had a secret hideaway.

She tried to watch where they were going, but she kept drifting from reality like a daydream, not knowing where they had traveled. Her mind was a whirl of questions, wondering who had found them, how they'd found them, and what would have happened had they been in a deep sleep instead of wide awake, almost making love on the couch?

Despite the anxiety about the night's events, Nevada's body still reacted to the images of Tyler hovering over her, touching her in ways she'd never been touched, eliciting responses from her she'd never given another man.

She allowed herself a brief moment of regret at the untimely interruption. What might have happened between them?

The Gateway Arch loomed closer as they approached downtown St. Louis. He lived somewhere in the heart of the city. Someplace no one knew about.

Except her. Nevada had just been given a huge gift.

Tyler Call's trust.

Chapter Seven

🕉

It was almost dawn by the time they arrived and the idea of sleep wasn't appealing in the least. Nevada was consumed with questions about the men who wanted to kill them.

Besides, she was completely blown away by the size of his condominium. On the twentieth floor of the most prestigious residential apartment building in the downtown area, Tyler's place had a panoramic view of every landmark, including the Gateway Arch and Mississippi River. To say she'd been stunned would be an understatement.

"The men who broke in were with the drug cartel," Tyler said as he handed Nevada a cup of coffee.

She murmured her thanks and tucked her feet under her on the plush couch in the oversized living room. "How do you know that?"

He smiled. "It's my job to know. I got enough of a glimpse of them to see a couple familiar faces I'd been tracking before. Guys from the warehouse."

"Who could have told them?" She took a sip, comforted by the warmth of the cup against her hands. Hopefully it would replace the chills she'd felt for the past few hours. Several sips later, she placed the coffee on the table next to her and grabbed the notebook and pen Tyler had given her. They had work to do.

"My first thought was that my internet connection had been hacked. But that's just not possible. It couldn't be an internet tracking system, because I'm on a private server with enough security our own government couldn't breach it. So it had to be someone at the agency who knew about what happened and that you were with me. Someone inside sold you out, sold us out."

Dread dropped her heart to her feet, her mind whirling with the possibility that someone at the NCA was a traitor.

It wouldn't do any good to dwell on the fact they could have been killed last night, or that in the space of a few days, she'd been constantly on the run for her life. Now they were both running and Tyler didn't trust the agency any longer. That meant she had to rely on him and him alone to keep her alive.

For someone who'd taken care of herself since she'd been barely adult, that was a bitter pill to swallow. She had to learn to do this herself. Despite her reservations about Tyler, both personal and professional, she needed to rely on him right now.

He was her teacher. At least professionally.

She shuddered at the images flitting across her mind. Images of personal things he could teach her. Her response to him back at the other house was enough for her to know she had much to learn about sex and men.

About this man.

He shrugged and leaned back against the plump cushions of the easy chair, his bare feet propped on the table. "There weren't that many people who knew you were with me, or who knew about my place in the country."

"Then let's start there. Name them."

"Legend, of course." Tyler pulled his hand through his dark hair. "I can't believe he'd be working against the agency. He's as devoted as they come."

"That may be what you think, but you know as well as I do that some of the most trustworthy and loyal agents have turned bad before."

He grimaced. "I know."

"Are you and Legend friends?"

"I thought we were. But friendship and business are two different things. And money changes people."

She caught the glimpse of disbelief followed by his sigh of resignation.

"Either way, he goes on the list of possibles," he said, his facial expression scrunched as if he found the very thought distasteful. "All right. Next on the list would be anyone who had access to the commander's files or was close enough to either him or Legend to know what had gone down at the warehouse."

They made the list, which included the assistant commander, a handful of other field agents and high-security-clearance analysts.

"Who else? Surely not the commander."

He threw a sharp glance at her. "Why not the commander? Right now, we're simply making a list of who had the knowledge of your whereabouts as well as my address. Commander Webster had both, so he goes on the list."

She nodded and wrote their superior's name down. "I can't believe he'd turn bad."

"Like you said, it happens to even the best agents. I don't want to assume anything," he said as he rose and motioned for her to follow him into the kitchen. "If we start trying to eliminate suspects based on our personal perceptions, it could get us killed."

He pulled a frying pan out of the long pantry in the brightly lit kitchen. White tile countertops and pale ash cabinets gave the room a cheery look. The stainless steel appliances added shine to the already luminous area.

"Eggs?"

She nodded.

"How?"

"Any way you're fixing them." She busied herself by making toast and pouring orange juice while Tyler worked on the eggs and bacon. They ate at the glass kitchen table nestled in a cozy nook overlooking the river. The tiny white blinds were half drawn to shut out the glare of the sun rising outside the bay windows. It was going to be hot again today.

Sitting here with Tyler seemed natural, comfortable. They were eating breakfast together, talking about their day. Okay, that part wasn't natural, but the rest of it was. Not many couples had days like they'd been having lately.

Couples. Why had her mind compartmentalized them that way? She forced the thought away. That's what happened when she spent too much time inside. Too much time to think.

Nevada loved being outdoors. Despite the sometimes overwhelming humidity, she loved fresh air and sunshine. Now she felt cooped up, unsettled—more like a prisoner than someone being protected.

And she sure as hell hadn't been given any training yet. Unless the command to run for her life constituted training.

She was getting pretty damn good at that. But eventually she'd have to stop running. Eventually she'd have to face the bad guys and she'd damn well better know how to deal with them when that day arrived.

She watched Tyler read the paper and sip his coffee. The morning sun highlighted his almost blue-black hair, which currently tipped rakishly over his forehead. Whenever he glanced at her, his dark eyes heated her more than the rays of sun peeking through the half-closed blinds.

She might have been a prisoner but she had the most devastatingly handsome prison guard on the face of the earth. It could have been much worse. She could have been stuck with an agent named Bubba—short, fat, balding and stupid. Yes, her situation could be a lot worse.

"So, now that we've narrowed down the list of possibles to people working at the agency, what's next? How do we figure out who's the inside man?"

He scooped a forkful of eggs and drank his orange juice in two gulps. "That should be pretty easy. I finish the mission. First, I'll drop a few clues about what I'm doing and see who comes after me."

Dread shot over her like black-edged lightning. The risks Tyler took frightened her more than she would ever admit to him. It was his job to take these risks. And she had no personal stake in his life anyway, so it shouldn't bother her. "In other words, whoever tries to kill you is the bad guy?"

And yet, even as the words spilled from her mouth, she knew it did bother her.

His smile didn't match the grim look in his eyes. "Something like that."

Her breakfast rolled in her stomach, that queasy feeling of fear beginning to escalate inside her. She couldn't—no, wouldn't—think about the danger he put himself in. "And you think you can finish the mission without someone to back you up?" She took their dishes to the sink and began to load the dishwasher.

"I usually work alone." He stood and cleared the table.

Nevada turned toward him and leaned against the sink, grabbing his arm as he walked by. "You're not alone now."

Their eyes met, so much unsettled between them. She feared for him, unhappy that he'd put his life in danger for a stupid mission. But that's what he did—it was his job. Whether she liked it or not. Besides, she had no right to like or dislike anything he did. She had no control over his life.

An easy smile played on his mouth. "You're not quite agent backup material yet."

Ignoring the immediate bristling at his remark, she replied coolly, "I could be if you'd give me some training."

He shook his head. "What I need to teach you isn't going to happen in a few days. Training takes time. We don't have that kind of time right now."

"I learn fast."

"Not that fast."

Refusing to back down, she said, "Then I can help you in other ways."

He lifted a tendril of hair off her shoulder, rubbing it between his thumb and middle finger.

She shivered and remembered the way his hands had glided over her body, the way she'd arched up to meet them, offering herself to him.

"Yes, I know how helpful you can be."

He wasn't referring to her analytical abilities. "I meant with the investigation."

"Oh, did you?"

He slid his palm behind her head, cupping her neck and drawing her lips to his. Without hesitating, she reached for him; wet, soapy palms splayed against his chest.

His heart thrummed against her palm in an ever-increasing beat. The confusion she normally felt around him always seemed to dim whenever he kissed her. Then, at least, everything felt right. Was that good or bad?

"The hot water's running," she murmured against his lips.

"Yes it is," he replied softly, then slid his mouth over her jaw and neck, playfully nipping at her shoulder.

The sensuous contact of teeth against skin made her gasp, her nipples pebbling against the thin cotton of her T-shirt. Instinctively she leaned into Tyler's bare chest, as if the mere act of pressing her aching breasts against him would offer relief.

He lifted his head to whisper teasingly in her ear. "Is the hot water making you cold?"

"Not at all." She leaned back and met his heated gaze.

He tilted her chin, forcing her eyes to meet his. "Then I take your hard nipples as a compliment." He kissed her mouth briefly and left the room. Nevada watched him with a hunger that never went away.

It took her all of an hour to figure out the kissing scene in the kitchen had been nothing more than a way to distract her. She'd mentioned helping him and he'd kissed her until she'd forgotten their conversation.

Well, not quite. That discussion wasn't over and she intended to bring it up again right away.

Except he was in the shower. Nevada sat on the bed in the spare bedroom, the sunlight pouring in from the windows and heating her skin. She needed a shower too, but once again she was without spare clothes. The shorts and shirt she'd thrown on last night in their hurry to escape were her only attire.

At least she had some privacy now, and even her own shower right outside her bedroom. But is that what she wanted? Privacy? Seemed last night she was willing to give up more than her privacy while she lay practically naked under Tyler.

Thinking about the things they'd done heated her even more than the streaming sunshine, sending sparks of desire jittering through her. She felt antsy, nervous and unsettled. How many life-changing events could a person handle in a few short days?

Never before had she craved intrigue and the heart-palpitating rush of adrenaline brought on by danger. Now she lived on the edge of danger, risking both her life and her heart. She wasn't sure what scared her most—the threat of the cartel wanting to kill her or the danger to her heart from a man whose voice sent shivers of sexual awareness through her body.

It was easier when Tyler was nothing but a fantasy—a dream about something that could never be. Then it was safe. Now, that fantasy had become a reality.

Suddenly the door to his bedroom opened and she stiffened, trying to look busy. Yeah, right. Busy doing what? Examining the ceiling? So, she'd been visualizing him naked—there was no crime in that.

"What are you thinking about?" he said as he crossed the hall and leaned against the doorway to her room.

If he continued to dress like that, her tension was going to escalate until she erupted like a boiling volcano. Clad only in a pair of cotton workout shorts, he could star in any woman's fantasy. Tan, tall and not an ounce of fat on him, his hair was still damp from the shower, uncombed in a just-had-sex kind of way.

Manipulation. That's what it was, pure and simple. He may have fooled her once, but not again. "I was thinking about the way you maneuvered me in the kitchen this morning."

"Maneuvered? How?"

She didn't buy his shocked look. "You kissed me."

"I didn't know kissing was considered manipulation," he said, one eyebrow elevated, lending him that sexy, hellion look. He viewed her through heavily lidded eyes. Bedroom eyes. If she were the swooning type of girl, she'd be collapsing about now. As it was, he made her heart want to leap out of her chest and attach itself to his.

"Well, you did." She rose from the bed and approached him, intending to stand firm in her desire to continue their earlier discussion. But then she made a fatal mistake. She inhaled.

How could plain soap smell so sexy on a man? He was fresh, clean and she was struck by a burning desire to lick that spot on his neck where a droplet of water rested.

"And how, exactly, did I do that?"

Her focus drifted back to his face and away from further temptation. "We were talking about me helping you and the next thing I knew you were kissing me, making me forget all about our conversation."

"Uh-huh. As if I had the capability to distract you," he said, trailing a finger along her cheek and down her neck, ever so slowly sliding down over her frantically beating heart.

"No, you don't." She grabbed his hand and pushed it away before he tricked her again. "I'm not dumb enough to let you do that to me twice."

"How about just once, then?"

Nevada knew he was talking about more than simple distraction. Damn if she couldn't feel her blood boiling at the thought. "Let's talk about how I can help you."

"I thought we just were." Now he was grinning like an idiot.

"Tyler!"

He threw his head back and laughed. "Okay, let's talk about it."

They went into the office, actually a small, recessed area off the main living room. An L-shaped desk housed a laptop and printer, along with Tyler's security system. Bright red lights scanned silently, their even lines providing a small measure of comfort after yesterday's upheaval.

She pulled up a chair in front of the monitor and connected to the Internet, while Tyler explained what needed to be done.

"How come no one knows about this place?" she asked.

"It's not in my name and I always have a safe house. The only ones who know about this condo are my parents and I think they can be trusted," he said with a wink.

"How come it's clean and has a newspaper and fully stocked kitchen?"

"I have paid help who keep it that way. I'm usually in and out of here a couple times a week. When I'm on long-term assignment, I let the help know so they don't buy fresh food."

There was a lot to learn about this secret agent business.

"We need to find out when and where the next shipment of supplies is coming in."

"Supplies to make methamphetamine?"

He nodded.

"Okay," she said as the connection was made and she entered the address for the search engine. "Explain the operation to me and I'll try to find what we need."

Tyler took a seat next to her, his fresh scent wafting over her in sensuous waves. *Concentrate.* She kept her gaze focused on the laptop.

"Meth labs are usually small operations; your average mom-and-pop drug manufacturers using common household products and appliances to create the drug."

"What chemicals do they use?"

"Lots of different kinds, like cleaning fluids, acetone and lantern fuel. Mainly, they use diet pills and cold medicine."

"Diet pills and cold medicine? What do they have to do with making illegal drugs?"

"There are two ways to cook meth. One is P-2-P, a shortened form of a lengthy chemical name. P-2-P is used by the big drug cartels in Mexico to manufacture meth."

"But not in the US?"

"It used to be, until our government restricted its use and distribution. Because of that, people wanting to make meth turned to another way called ephedrine reduction."

"Isn't ephedrine an ingredient in cold medicines?"

"Yeah, and diet pills. The meth cooks have to extract the ephedrine from over-the-counter cold medicines. Which is why most meth labs have been small operations."

She frowned. "I don't understand."

Tyler took her hand in his. She felt the stirring of her pulse as he rubbed his fingers over the base of her thumb.

"It takes a very large amount of ephedrine to make a very small amount of meth. The government is aware of what local meth makers do—they buy ephedrine in bulk from the drugstore. That practice has been banned. Now drug and grocery stores limit the number of packages of cold medicines that can be sold to one person."

As if he just realized he was holding her hand, Tyler released it and rose from the table. "More coffee?"

She nodded and watched him leave the room, then turned back to the laptop to begin her search. By the time he returned with their coffee cups, she was full of questions. "So the drug cartel in Mexico brings in the P-2-P instead, setting up larger operations which can manufacturer bigger quantities of meth."

"Right. And larger operations mean more meth on the street. They're sophisticating the drug manufacturing and distribution by eliminating the little people who bought ephedrine at the store and made meth in their garage."

"I had no idea," she said, shocked at what little she knew about such a dangerous drug.

"Meth is profitable. The more they make, the more they sell. The more they sell, the more people they get addicted."

"And more addicts equals increased sales." She shuddered at the thought.

He nodded. "Which is why we have to stop this influx of chemicals and put a halt to the start-up of these regional distribution networks."

"Then let's get started." Armed with determination, Nevada vowed whatever they needed, she'd find it.

* * * * *

Tyler had left the condo hours ago. Nevada had been hard at work, looking for clues to the impending shipment of supplies. She'd waved him off when he said he had to leave for a bit.

It bugged the hell out of him that someone in the agency sold them out, knowing the cartel would have them killed.

As he shut the front door and set the security system, he pulled out his cell phone, noting several calls from both the commander and Dylan, as well as other field agents. Calls he wouldn't return. Not just yet.

By now they'd know he and Nevada had left his house in the country. If someone at the NCA wasn't in on the plan to kill them, they'd be frantically trying to reach him. Either way, until he discovered who was working against the agency, he wasn't going to make contact with anyone.

Someone inside the NCA was involved with the drug cartel.

But who? And why? For money? Or something else?

He and Dylan went back quite a few years. His gut told him Dylan was innocent. Dylan sure as hell didn't need the money, so it didn't make sense for him to be in with the cartel. But logic forced him to consider everyone, no matter his personal feelings.

Nevada barely looked up from the laptop screen when he came in the door. He said hello as he passed by and all he got was a brief wave in his general direction.

He threw the bags down in her room and walked out, waiting for her to notice him.

"Find anything?" he asked as he approached her.

No answer.

"Nevada."

He had to give her credit for her ability to concentrate.

"Nevada!"

Glaring eyes popped over the top of the monitor. "You don't have to shout. What is it?"

"Did you find anything?"

"Sort of."

Well, there's a definitive answer. "I bought you some clothes while I was out."

"That's nice."

She wasn't listening to him.

"Thought you might like a shower. You know, freshen up a bit."

"Sounds great."

When she concentrated, she really concentrated.

"I was thinking that after your shower you could suck my dick."

"Okay."

He suppressed the laugh.

"Maybe even do it twice."

Finally her head popped up. "Huh? Do what twice?"

He crossed his arms and leaned against the archway to the room, feeling victorious. "Too late now. You already agreed."

Her brows furrowed, confusion written all over her face. "Agreed? What are you talking about?"

"Our conversation. You just agreed to take a shower and blow me."

Her golden eyes widened in shock. "I did not!"

Then he couldn't help it. He laughed at her, which didn't seem to please her one bit. "When you concentrate, you agree to anything. I'll have to keep that in mind for future reference."

She stood and stretched her back, her breasts straining against her shirt. His gaze was riveted to the sharp points poking the thin material, wishing he could flick his thumbs over her distended nipples.

"Sorry. I was working. I've found a few things that might interest you. But the shower sounds like a great idea. I'll be right back."

He nodded and sat in front of the monitor to peruse the information on the screen when he heard her bedroom door open. He looked up and smiled at her stunned look.

"You bought me clothes."

"Yes, I believe I mentioned that when I came back, but you were too busy to notice."

"And they're all the right size. How did you know?"

"I guessed."

"Guessed?"

"Yeah." He wasn't about to tell her he noticed what sizes she bought when he took her shopping. Definitely not a guy thing.

Her face colored, which he found adorable. Not many women blushed these days. The fact that she did turned him on quicker than if she'd done a naked table dance.

Although the naked table dance sounded intriguing too.

"Thank you," she said as she stood awkwardly between the hall and the office. "I appreciate you thinking of me."

"You're welcome."

"I'm going to take that shower now."

"Okay."

She didn't break eye contact and neither did he. Finally, she turned and walked into her bedroom without another word.

And then he exhaled.

God, she was making him crazy. The last thing in the world he needed right now was an attraction to the woman he was supposed to protect and train. Yet there it was, as obvious as his constant state of discomfort whenever she was near.

He didn't want this, but damn if he wasn't getting tired of trying to fight it.

Be serious, he told himself. Just when, exactly, had he tried to fight her off? When he'd taken her in his arms and kissed her, or when he had her half-naked underneath him? Obviously she was such a brute she'd overpowered him, forcing herself under him. He laughed out loud at the visual.

He wanted her so damn bad his hands shook like an addict needing a fix. And Nevada was the drug.

His feelings for her were compromising the mission, making him lose his focus. Time was dwindling and the stakes were increasing. Taking out this cartel had to be first on his mind.

Not the desire to make love to the woman whose every word, every movement, every touch, threatened to take him to a place he'd never been. The logical thing to do would be to get her out of his life, and out of his mind, as soon as possible.

But how? It's not like he could contact the NCA and make arrangements for someone else to take her. That would be a surefire way to get her killed.

He needed someone he could trust. Someone he knew she'd be safe with.

Then it hit him and he grinned. Perfect. Not only would the plan alleviate him of his bodyguard duties, it would give him an opportunity to brainstorm ideas about the cartel and the insider at the agency.

Tyler had a plan. The perfect plan.

Chapter Eight

෨

"Tell me again why we're going to your parents' house?" Nevada fidgeted, feeling ridiculous about being nervous. She wasn't his girlfriend. This was a mission. She was a coworker.

"I need to talk to my dad about what's going on at the agency."

"Couldn't you just call him on the phone?"

"No. I don't trust the phones."

They'd left the condo early, after Tyler rousted her from a less-than-restful sleep to inform her they were going to his parents'. She'd barely had time to throw on clothes and make herself presentable before he dragged her out the front door.

Men. They could shower and dress in ten minutes. Didn't they understand how long it took a woman to look decent? Thankfully she'd showered the night before, so all she had to do was braid her hair and toss on the khaki shorts and marine green tank top she'd set out the night before.

They headed south, out of the city. He kept a watchful eye on the rearview mirror, checking to make sure they weren't being followed.

A short drive later they'd crossed the Missouri River and Tyler exited the freeway, heading toward the more affluent areas outside the city limits. Nevada was awed by the size of the homes and land. Having lived in an apartment for so many years, these beautiful homes astounded her.

Tyler pulled up to a gated community, greeted the guard and told him he was there to see Edward and Margaret Call.

The guard phoned, then pressed a button and told him to drive through.

Giant birch trees lined the wide, winding streets. Each massive-sized house had its own unique architectural style. Nevada peered through the darkened glass of the SUV and imagined living in a place like this with a loving husband and house full of kids.

Where had that come from? She quickly turned to face front, shocked at her own thoughts. Husband, home and family weren't things she daydreamed about. After losing her parents, the last thing she wanted was to risk loving someone, only to have that love ruthlessly wrenched from her grasp.

Besides, she was happy being single. She had her career and for now that's all she needed.

Yeah, right. If that was true, why did she suddenly have this vision of a home in the suburbs, a handsome husband with midnight eyes and a scattering of beautiful children at her feet?

Stress. Had to be stress and being forced to share space with a hot, sexy man she'd been fantasizing about for months. And she hadn't slept well lately, either.

She shook off the images as Tyler pulled into a long driveway. A huge Victorian loomed ahead, its square lines and almost flat roof looking very regimented, yet elegant.

Taking Tyler's lead, she exited the SUV and followed him to the covered porch. The tall columns on either side of the stairs stood at attention like well-trained military guards.

He knocked, which she found unusual. Wouldn't he simply walk in? This was, after all, his parents' house. Wasn't it his home too?

It didn't take long for the door to be answered by a petite woman with short blonde hair and warm brown eyes. This must be Tyler's mother.

"Tyler!" she exclaimed and threw her arms around her son, who easily lifted his mother off the ground in a bear hug.

"Hey, Mom," he said, kissing her on the cheek. Sliding his arm around his mother's waist, he turned to Nevada. "Mom, this is Nevada James. Nevada, my mother, Margaret Call."

"I'm so pleased to meet you, Nevada," she said enthusiastically as she held out her hand.

"Nice to meet you too, Mrs. Call," Nevada replied, trying to quell the ridiculous butterflies running rampant through her already jittery stomach.

"Call me Margaret." His mother stood aside to let them enter.

Nevada stepped into the large entry and followed Tyler and his mother into the living area.

"Your home is lovely, Margaret." Nevada settled into a Queen Anne chair. The furnishings matched the home, everything decorated in dark wood and complimentary colors of mauve and brown. A dark stone fireplace centered the living area, flanked on either side by two plush couches and a heavy coffee table.

"Thank you," Margaret sat next to Tyler. Grasping his hands, she smiled lovingly at him. "What are you doing here today?"

"I need to talk to Dad. Is he here?"

She shook her head. "Playing golf. But he should be back shortly. How about some iced tea?" she asked, looking at them both.

Nevada turned her eyes to Tyler. He smiled and nodded at his mother.

They followed her into the homey kitchen, decorated in bright yellow buttercups, from the eyelet curtains over the back door and kitchen window to the tiny patterns on the white and yellow floor. Nevada fell in love with the charm and comfort of the room.

"Let me help you," Nevada offered.

"Nonsense, you're a guest," Margaret replied with a wave of her hand. "Go. Sit at the table with Tyler."

The woman was certainly energetic, flitting around the kitchen, preparing iced tea, setting out sugar, lemon and even freshly baked cookies. Nevada suddenly felt very undomesticated.

"What have you been up to, Mom?"

Her brown eyes sparkled as she smiled at her son. "Oh, you know, the same thing all the time. Taking care of your father and the house, doing a little shopping, playing some bridge."

Tyler leaned back in the chair. "Still whoopin' Dad's ass on a regular basis in bridge?"

Margaret tapped his hand. "Mind your language, young man." Then she laughed, the cutest little-girl giggle Nevada had ever heard. "Well, yes. As a matter of fact, I am."

Margaret Call had a feisty streak underneath that perfect wife and mother exterior.

"Tell me, Nevada, what brings you along with Tyler today?"

Uh-oh. How was she supposed to answer that one? How much did his mother know about the agency, about her son's line of work?

She quickly looked to Tyler, who appeared as clueless as she how to answer Margaret's question. She started to speak, figuring she'd wing it, but Tyler interrupted.

"Actually, we've been dating for a little while."

Margaret's mouth opened in surprise. "Dating? You?"

Nevada's mouth followed, hanging open like a fish waiting for a hook.

Margaret gaped at her son as if she couldn't believe he would ever bring a date home. And making it even more interesting was Tyler's look of growing discomfort. He fidgeted and ran his hand through his hair.

"Yeah, dating."

His mother raised her eyebrows and Nevada did her best to hide her smile behind the glass of tea she sipped.

"What? I date!"

Margaret nodded. "Uh-huh. When was the last time you brought a girl home? Senior prom in high school?"

Tyler choked on his tea. "Mom," he protested, while trying to clear his throat.

Margaret sat back with a smug look on her face.

Nevada was so glad they came. Here was an insight into Tyler she'd never seen. The sexiest, most arrogantly confident and powerful man she'd ever met, reduced to babbling like a toddler after one comment from his mother. Priceless.

"Come around here more often, Nevada, and you'll learn all the deep, dark secrets about my son." She took Nevada's hand. "It's nice to see he finally found a girl to bring home."

If only it were true, instead of the lie Tyler made up to hide his job and her reason for accompanying him. But it could never be. Could never work, for either of them. For so many reasons.

"Thank you," she said. "I'm very happy to be here." Surprisingly, that part wasn't a lie. Having lived without a mother for the past ten years, she felt comforted by the warmth of a maternal hand. Margaret was extremely likeable.

Tyler cleared his throat and Nevada glanced over to see the frown on his face. Now what had she done?

Margaret caught the look. "Excuse me for a moment. I have something to do upstairs. I'll be right back."

"What?" Nevada asked as soon as Margaret was out of earshot.

"Sorry. I didn't know what else to say and I'd like to keep my mother as uninvolved in my business as possible."

She shrugged. "I kind of figured you weren't seriously declaring your undying love for me in front of your mother."

"Did you want me to?"

Where had *that* come from? Tyler cringed inwardly as soon as the words fell out of his mouth. From the look of shock on her face, Nevada was just as surprised as he.

"Wh…what?"

Great. She was probably going to run screaming from the house now. He wanted to beat his head against the kitchen table, hoping it would rearrange the obviously jumbled gray matter inside. What had he been thinking? He didn't love Nevada. He didn't have time for love.

"I was just kidding. Of course you didn't want me to. Just trying to lighten things up." *Nice backtracking, Call.*

"Oh."

He heard the hurt in her simple reply. Damn. When he rose and approached her, she leaned back in the chair as if she could slink under the table and avoid him altogether.

"Stand up, Nevada."

Her eyes were wide pools. She shook her head. "This isn't a good idea, Tyler."

"Stand up."

Again, that negative shake.

Exasperated, he grasped her hands and pulled her to her feet, forcing her to stand in front of him when she would have backed away.

"Look at me."

She did. Right at his chest. He tilted her chin until those golden eyes met his.

"I'm sorry. I hurt you."

"Don't be silly. You didn't hurt me at all."

She didn't lie very well, despite her shrug of indifference. Pain shimmered near the surface of her eyes, the corners crinkling with barely suppressed anguish.

"Yeah, I did. I don't know how, but I did."

"Tyler, you didn't hurt me. I know why we're here and what we're not. We're not a couple, we're not in love. I think sometimes we don't even like each other. I mean, it's not as if we'd been dating or anything. We haven't. There's nothing between us. I know it and you know it. We have a job to do and I'm a guest you didn't want to have to deal with. You had to lie to your mother. I understand that. After all, your job is at stake and—"

"You talk too much," he interrupted, pulling her into his arms and silencing her litany with a kiss.

His head spun at the touch of her mouth. Her lips parted and she accepted his tongue eagerly, matching his frantic stroking with her own. God, she made him crazy. He wrapped his arms around her tighter, letting her feel how involved he really was. One touch of his lips against hers and he was hard and ready in an instant.

That's how much he didn't care. If they were alone he'd already have her half-naked and spread out on the kitchen table. He never craved a woman before, never had one on his mind constantly, never really cared how they felt one way or another.

It was different with Nevada. Her soft moans and the way she pressed herself so intimately against him drove him up the wall. If only they were alone.

"Ahem."

They weren't. At the sound of a clearing throat, Nevada pulled away from Tyler like he'd just set her on fire. He had to keep his back turned for a few seconds to settle his composure, among other things.

"Sorry, didn't know the kitchen was occupied."

This was horrible. Nevada was mortified. Caught kissing in the kitchen like a couple of kids. And by a stern-looking gentleman in golf attire who had to be Tyler's father.

"Hey, Dad." Tyler turned away from her, but not before she caught the quick glimpse of regret in his eyes.

"Son." His eyes sparkled with an amused glint as he shook Tyler's hand.

Didn't they hug each other? Was that a man thing, or something else?

Tyler turned to her. "Nevada James, this is my father, Edward Call."

She shook his hand, struck by the uncanny resemblance between father and son. If it weren't for the age difference and the fact Edward Call's hair was more silver than midnight black, they could have been brothers. "I'm pleased to meet you, Mr. Call."

"Most people call me either Edward or General." He smiled. "Old Marines never retire, you know."

Edward, like Margaret, was trim, fit and looked the picture of health, not at all his age, which, if she remembered what Tyler told her on the drive, was somewhere in his late sixties. He had the same serious look that Tyler always wore. Now she knew where he got it.

"So what brings you our way today?" Edward fixed a glass of tea and sat at the table.

"I need your help."

Edward showed no emotion. "What kind of help?"

"An agency thing. Something's come up and I need your opinion."

"Can't handle it by yourself?"

Ouch. That sounded like an inference of incompetence. She watched for Tyler's reaction, but the question didn't seem to bother him. He must be used to his father's gruff personality.

"Yes, sir, I can handle it. I just wanted to ask you a couple questions."

Edward nodded. "Fine, then. Let's go to my office." He stood and left the room without another word.

She started to follow, but Tyler pressed a hand to her shoulder and stopped her. "I'll be right back."

"If it's agency business I should go with you."

"I'll fill you in later."

Irritation had her clenching her teeth. "Don't shut me out of this, Tyler."

He rolled his eyes. "I don't have time for this. Just stay put and I'll be right back." He turned and walked out and she dropped into a chair and crossed her arms.

How the hell was she supposed to learn anything if he kept her out of the loop? Dammit, if this wasn't his parents home she'd have stormed right after them, refusing to be put off. But if Tyler didn't want his mother to know about the agency business, she couldn't very well cause a scene.

Damn him. He knew that. He knew she wouldn't put up too much of a fight.

"So the men up and left you, did they?"

Nevada looked up as Margaret entered the kitchen. "Yes, they did."

She smiled indulgently. "They do that to me, too. All the time. Edward likes to secret himself in his office whenever there's talk of military business. Tyler's the same way whenever something comes up with his work at the agency."

Well, knock her over with a stick! "You know about the agency?"

Margaret's eyes crinkled at the corners when she grinned. "Honey, there isn't a whole lot I don't know." She inclined her head toward the hallway where Tyler and his father had disappeared. "They just think I don't know anything."

Nevada couldn't be more shocked. "Do they…"

"Do they know that I know?" she said with a laugh. "Truthfully, I have no idea. But it makes them feel better to think they're protecting me, so I let them. Men are somewhat clueless when it comes to how much internal strength women possess."

"You are *so* right about that," Nevada agreed, completely floored by Tyler's mother. This tiny woman, who appeared the domestic, mild mannered, straight-out-of-a-fifties-sitcom type, was actually much stronger than she'd ever surmised.

"Just like I know that you are not simply some girl Tyler is dating. Do you work with him at the agency?"

Stunned, all Nevada could do was nod truthfully. "I'm an analyst…err, actually I'm an agent in training."

"I see. And you're helping him with a case?"

"You could say that." *Tyler, where are you? Hellllp!*

"So, tell me, dear," Margaret said as she poured them both another glass of tea. "Are you and Tyler having sex, or has your relationship not progressed that far yet?"

If Margaret kept this up Nevada was going to have a heart attack before Tyler returned from his father's office.

"Are we having...oh no, no, ma'am, not at all!" Her heart pounded with guilt as if she'd just been caught doing the deed in front of his mother. Actually she wasn't lying. They weren't having sex. Not yet, anyway. But she'd like to think that someday, maybe...

Margaret leveled her gaze at Nevada. "Oh, come now. This isn't the dark ages. You and Tyler can't keep your eyes off each other. I know my son and I can see he has feelings for you."

Okay, maybe she would have to reassess Margaret's keen insight. She was clearly way off the mark on this one. "There's nothing between Tyler and me. We just work together."

Margaret leveled an honest look at her. "Like I said. I know Tyler. I know how he is, what he likes and doesn't like. He's never brought a woman here before, business or otherwise."

She started to interject but Margaret held up her hand to prevent it.

"I saw the way he looked at you earlier." Her eyebrow arched in an all-knowing-mother kind of look. "Believe me, I know when a man's attracted." She smoothed her short hair and grinned. "I was quite a looker in my day."

Nevada couldn't help but grin back. "You still are."

"Thanks, but I wasn't fishing for compliments. What I mean is, I know the look on a man's face when he's in love. My son is in love with you. Last time I saw that look was in high school, when he fell head over heels for Cynthia Lake, who promptly dumped him for an older college boy."

How was she supposed to respond to that? "I...don't think he is."

"Then you're blind. Open your eyes and take a gander at the way he looks at you. If you're as smart as I think you are, you'll see it too."

The telephone rang. Saved by the bell never seemed more appropriate than at that moment. Margaret excused herself and took the call.

In love with her? No way. They'd only met a few days ago and since then their relationship had been anything but ordinary. Add the fact they were both running for their lives to the mix and it was easy to see that what they had was a shared goal and nothing more. They both wanted to stay alive.

And, of course, Tyler's primary goal was to bring down the cartel. No matter what.

But in love? She snorted. Hardly. He wasn't any more in love with her than she was with him. They merely shared close proximity and a kind of nervous excitement. And a definite sexual attraction that had everything to do with chemistry and nothing to do with emotion. That was all.

"Well, that was interesting," Margaret said as she returned to the kitchen.

"What's that?"

"The telephone call." Margaret looked down the long hallway. Nevada waited and figured she'd tell her about the call when she was ready. "That was Tyler on the telephone."

Now she was confused. "Tyler? But he's in the office with his father."

Margaret's lips curled and she shrugged. "Not any more. He and Edward went out to do some *shopping*, as they called it. Which means they're out doing some cloak and dagger stuff."

Out? He left? Now it was Nevada's turn to look down the hallway, as if somehow she could see the ghost trail of their departure. "Did he say when they'd be back?"

Margaret pulled a roast from the refrigerator. "Sometime tomorrow."

"What? Tomorrow? I don't understand." He left her here? Without a word as to where he was going?

"Yes. He said to tell you there's a bag at the front door with a change of clothes and some of your toiletries. He took the liberty of packing for you early this morning."

He packed for *her*. Her blood boiled. Left her! Dumped her here, like she was a child to be dropped at the babysitter! And worst of all, he'd planned this. All along, from the moment they woke this morning, he knew he was going to leave her here.

She stood and furiously paced the length of the kitchen. How dare he? In love with her? Ha! More likely he loathed her and couldn't wait to get rid of her. That's why he brought her here. To offload his burden, so he could concentrate all his efforts on the precious mission. That's what he was really in love with!

Dammit! How the hell was she supposed to become a field agent if he kept tossing her in a closet whenever something came up? Fury put her in a rage, adrenaline flowing freely through her bloodstream. She wanted to punch something, to scream at the top of her lungs. Goddamit, he pissed her off!

"Would you like to help me fix dinner, Nevada? Looks like it will just be the two of us tonight."

It was clear by Margaret's crooked grin she was well aware of Nevada's agitated state. Still, she didn't want to embarrass herself by calling Tyler all the derogatory names flowing through her mind right now. After all, Margaret was his mother. Calling Tyler an insensitive prick in front of his mother wasn't a good idea.

"Sure, I'd love to," she ground out between clenched teeth, trying to sound as cheerful as possible. Underneath, she was about to erupt. But she'd wait, enjoy dinner and Margaret's company. When Tyler came back tomorrow, she'd unleash everything she'd been forced to hold inside.

Tyler Call, look out! Hell hath no fury like a woman dumped.

Chapter Nine

☙

He hadn't worked on a case with his father in quite awhile. Not since his early days at the agency. Back then, his entire life had depended on making his father proud. At the time he joined the NCA, his dad was the commander and Tyler was fresh from his stint in the Marines.

"Find anything yet?" Tyler paced back and forth as Edward searched the military's database.

"Not yet. This trucking company, or whatever it is, has hidden their identities too well."

In order to avoid any contact with the NCA office in St. Louis, they'd driven to Kansas City to make use of the US government's massive search database. They'd spent all day and night probing, but had come up with nothing. Tyler had hoped the military database, with its sophisticated search capabilities, would be able to gather more information on the mystery trucking company than Nevada had.

"You said Nevada found the names of the principal owners of Mercado?"

He nodded and took a sip of what had to be his tenth cup of coffee. He wasn't even sure what time it was. Sometime in the early afternoon, he guessed. He could barely keep his eyes open. How did his father, a sixty-five-year-old man, go so long without sleep? The answer was beyond him, but then his father had always been tough.

"She's pretty damn skilled at her job, then, because she's way ahead of what we can do here."

That's what he figured. Not what he wanted to hear, but what he expected. "Yeah, she's good at research."

And it pissed him off that he needed her skills. He worked alone. Successfully. He didn't need a partner and he sure as hell didn't want to get any closer to Nevada than he already had. As it was he could barely keep his hands off her.

Getting away from her had been just what he needed. Spending time with his father had reminded him that he needed to focus on the mission, not on getting laid.

He and his dad were in a private office reserved for special visitors, seated side by side at a large folding table. The room was sparsely furnished, mainly used for research purposes. A massive computer took up most of the available desk space. His father's military connections opened a lot of doors that Tyler otherwise wouldn't be able to pass through.

"Thanks for your help, anyway." So much for dumping Nevada. He still needed her for her research capabilities. But that was all.

Yeah, right, Call. Keep telling yourself that and maybe you'll start to believe it.

"Are you sure about the agency?" Edward regarded him with disbelief.

Tyler shrugged. "Honestly, I don't know. But no one else knew Nevada was with me."

"I suppose. But I know Alan Webster. Hell, he worked under me when I was commander and in the Marines before that. I trust him with my life."

"I thought the same thing about Dylan, but I can't risk Nevada's life on it."

"Understandable." Edward paused a moment, then continued. "But I don't need to remind you the good of the mission is paramount. Sometimes sacrifices have to be made."

Had he heard his father correctly? "You mean it's okay to give up one person in order to break the case on the drug cartel? Or maybe even two people, myself included."

Edward frowned. "No, son, I'm not advocating you put yourself on the chopping block like that, nor am I saying the young lady is expendable. But the mission is the most important goal and that's where your loyalties should lie."

"They do."

Edward leaned back in the chair and crossed his hands in front of his stomach. "Do they? Have you given any thought to the possibility that you're protecting this girl at the cost of the mission? That maybe your motivations where she's concerned aren't entirely professional?"

Tyler turned in his chair, unable to believe what he was hearing. "What are you getting at?"

"Nothing. I just want you to think about this girl and what she means to you. If it's personal, if you're involved with her, it could affect your thinking."

"It's not personal."

Edward cast a disbelieving glance at him. "Think about it, that's all I'm saying."

He'd done nothing but think about it the rest of the day. And once they got in the car to head back to St. Louis, his father's words pervaded his mind, forcing all other thoughts aside.

Maybe it was because he'd gone without sleep for too long, but what his father said didn't settle right. *The mission was everything.* God, how many years had he heard that? Forever, it seemed. How many sacrifices had his father made in order to be successful? And bottom line — was it worth it?

Maybe to Edward Call, putting his work above everything else in his life *was* the most important thing. But was it worth it to Tyler?

He was tired. So damn tired he could hardly think anymore. How many years had he been doing this? Between military college, the Marines and the agency, it had been over twelve years. Had he ever paused to think about *why* he did it? Why he went into the Marines and why he ended up as an operative with the NCA?

The answer was simple and currently sat next to him in the car.

"Dad, can I ask you a question?"

"Sure. Shoot."

"All these years you were in the military and then with the NCA, did you ever miss having a regular job?"

"What do you mean?"

Tyler wrapped both hands around the steering wheel. "How much time did you travel during those years? How often were you away from home on a mission?" He already knew the answer, but he wanted to hear it from his father's viewpoint.

Edward shrugged. "I don't know. Never really paid much attention."

But Tyler had. All those years of worshiping his hero from afar, because it was the only choice he had. Dad was rarely around and, even when he was, his head was so wrapped around military life and missions that he didn't have much time to spend with his son. Or his wife, for that matter.

Had he failed to notice his father's absence all those years because his mother had been there, acting as both parents? And what about her life? She seemed happy, but what did a child really know about his parents? She could have been miserable every day her entire married life and he'd never have known any different, because she'd made sure he had everything he needed.

What had his mother sacrificed so his father could live his dream?

Is that what Tyler wanted? Would he wake up someday and realize he'd missed having a life? A family? Was he satisfied with his career being the love of his life, or did he want more?

He pondered the thought for a minute, until it became very clear to him.

Hell yes, he wanted more.

"What are you thinking about?"

It took him a few seconds to register that his father was talking to him.

"Nothing much. Why?"

"The look on your face."

"What about it?"

"You were concentrating. Like you'd just made some monumental decision." Edward offered a sly smile, as if he'd just been let in on a secret. "Thinking about the mission, aren't you?"

How could he have been so blind all these years? How could he not have seen what was so clearly right in front of his face the whole time? "Yeah, Dad, that's it. The mission."

"That's my boy. I knew if you thought about it for awhile, you'd come to your senses and get your priorities back on track." His father slapped him on the back. "I'm proud of you, son."

I'm proud of you, son.

Tyler forced away the raw pain that tore at his gut. All the years of wanting to hear those words spoken by his father and now they left him empty. Empty and feeling the need to have something more tangible in his life than a pat on the back from a man who thought an agency assignment was more important than a woman's life.

"Given any thoughts as to what your next step is going to be?" Edward asked.

Tyler studied the gleam in his father's eye. The old man lived for this—the danger, the excitement. It was all a game to him and he'd never tire of it.

"Yeah, I have a few ideas." The lights of St. Louis loomed ahead. Within a half hour they'd be back at his parents', and if he knew Nevada, he'd have one hell of a pissed off woman on his hands.

He had a few ideas. Definitely. But none of them had to do with the mission. He wondered what his father would think about his sudden shift in priorities, then dismissed the thought. Actually, he didn't care what his father thought. Not anymore.

* * * * *

Ten o'clock. She'd been here over thirty-six hours, virtually held prisoner. And poor Margaret probably felt like a babysitter. A babysitter to a woman on the edge.

At least Margaret was the bright spot in all of this. The woman was wonderful. Always cheerful, upbeat, with a wicked sense of humor. They'd laughed themselves to tears as Margaret regaled her with stories of Tyler's errant childhood.

If she had been Tyler's girlfriend, she'd have grabbed her pen and paper and taken notes. Margaret held nothing back, from spilling the beans that Tyler had sucked his thumb until he was six, to making them both laugh and redden in embarrassment at the time she'd caught her son, literally with his pants down, in the garage. Of course he was sixteen at the time, but the young lady in question had been at least twenty years old.

Margaret explained between hysterical fits of laughter that she'd taken comfort in the fact her son was being well schooled in the art of pleasing women.

"Gin."

"Dammit, Margaret, that's the fourth time in a row!" Nevada threw the cards down and glared at her.

Margaret shrugged innocently. "I just play the cards, dear. I can't help it if I win."

She tried to maintain her evil death stare, but couldn't keep her lips from curling in a crooked smile. "I think you cheat," she added as she finished off her glass of wine.

"Now, now, Nevada. Mustn't be a sore loser." Margaret downed her own glass of wine and gathered up the cards. "I don't know about you, but I'm beat. How about we call it a night?"

Great. Another night spent in Tyler's bedroom. Feeling him everywhere, inhaling his scent on the sheets as if he still occupied that room every night. "Sounds good to me." Nevada gathered up their wine glasses and rinsed them in the sink.

If she had to be dumped somewhere, at least it was with enjoyable company. Margaret was the closest thing to a mother she'd had in years. She already knew she'd miss her when they left.

That is, if he ever came back for her.

"He'll be back tonight. Don't worry." Margaret laid a hand on her arm and Nevada turned around, drying her hands on the dishtowel.

"How do you know he'll be back tonight?" It was as if the woman read her thoughts, knew her insecurities.

"I just do. Try and get some sleep."

Nevada nodded and Margaret turned to leave, then stopped.

"I've really enjoyed having you around."

Were those tears brimming in Margaret's eyes? Oh please don't do that, she thought as she felt the moisture welling in her own.

She picked up Margaret's hands, so small they almost fit inside hers. "I've enjoyed it too."

"You still miss your mother, don't you?"

Unable to trust that her voice wouldn't crack with emotion, she nodded. Margaret swept Nevada's hair back from her face, and planted a kiss on her cheek. "You're already like a daughter to me. Silly, I know."

She shook her head. "Oh no, it isn't silly at all. I feel it too."

Impulsively she wrapped her arms around the petite woman and hugged her.

"Good night, dear."

Nevada let out a shaky sigh. She hadn't realized how lonely she'd been until she spent the past couple days with Tyler's mother. Unable to take another devastating loss after her parents' deaths, she'd closed herself off from anyone she could possibly love. Which meant that, other than a handful of less-than-close friends and coworkers, she was alone.

Oh sure, she dated. Randomly, here and there. Even had a few so-called relationships. But whenever someone got too close, she ended it. Eventually she just stopped trying, afraid she'd meet the one person she was destined to be with. If she did, if there really was someone like that for her out there, she'd be too paralyzed with fear to ever act upon it. Which meant more loss and more pain. Better to remain alone than take that risk.

She trudged up the stairs and entered Tyler's room, unable to resist a smile as Margaret's stories came to mind. At least his mother hadn't left it the way it had been the day he left for college like some parents did, creating a shrine to their children's youth.

By the looks of things, this was a standard spare bedroom. A queen bed centered the room, with matching chests of drawers flanking either side. Pictures of Tyler from infancy through his years in the military littered the bookcase against the wall. She found herself drawn to those pictures, as if somehow they could give her some clue to the man she'd spent almost a week with.

A week and yet it seemed longer, as if they'd made an intimate connection that made time irrelevant.

She picked up his high school graduation picture, tracing his smiling, youthful face with her fingertip. He still had that mischievous, little boy grin, like in the picture. His eyes shone with the brightness of youth—that feeling of immortality, the blissful ignorance of thinking you alone could change the world.

"I can't believe she still has those pictures up."

She spun around, shocked to hear Tyler's voice behind her. He stood in the doorway, the mere sight of him enough to make her breath catch in her throat.

She was so damn glad he was back she wanted to throw her arms around him. And she was so pissed off at being dumped she wanted to kick him in the balls.

"Miss me?"

Trying desperately to avoid showing the joy she felt at his return, she willed her anger back, full force. She shot him her most scathing look. "Miss you? Hardly."

"Oh, come on, Nevada," he said as he entered the room and closed the door behind him. "Admit it. You were lonely without me around."

"Actually, I wasn't." She replaced his picture on the chest and crossed the room, intending to close herself in the bathroom until she was able to get her riotous emotions under control. And when she did, they'd talk. But not right now. Not when one part of her wanted to kill him and the other part wanted to lick every inch of his body.

He grabbed her upper arm as she walked by, halting her escape. She looked at his hand and then met his eyes. "Let go of me."

He released her arm. "Where are you going?"

Was he oblivious to her anger? "I'm going to get ready for bed."

He pursed his lips and arched a dark eyebrow. "Really? Okay, I'll wait."

She shook her head. "Not okay. You'll leave." She pointed to the door just in case he didn't know where it was.

"Uh-uh. This is my room."

"Not tonight it isn't."

"Yes, tonight it is. As it is every time I come here."

She crossed her arms in front of her and offered him a smug smile. "You don't really want me to call your mother to mediate this argument, do you?" She felt empowered after bonding with Margaret. Blood relative or not, she'd take Nevada's side against Tyler.

"Go ahead. Dad's a little grouchy when you wake him up, so knock gently." He moved out of her way so she could open the door.

Damn him for calling her bluff. No way in hell was she going to act like a five year old and shout for Tyler's mother at the top of her lungs.

"Well?"

"Well what?" How was she going to get out of this one?

"I'm waiting for you to get my mother to referee. Or will you just cry uncle now and be done with it?"

She threw out a laugh. "You don't seriously expect me to sleep in this room with you tonight, do you?"

His eyes darkened and she felt the heat shoot from him to her in an instant. "Oh, we won't be sleeping."

The audacity of the man. "Let me set a few things straight with you," she said, her ire rising by the millisecond. "First, you dump me here without explaining a damn thing to me, and then you return a day and a half later and announce we'll be sleeping together. Don't you find that a bit presumptuous?"

He cocked a crooked grin. "No."

She pointed a finger at his chest. "And speaking of dumping me, where the hell did you go and why didn't you take me with you? Or at least tell me what the plan was?" She advanced on him, backing him further and further toward the closed door until he was pressed against it. "Do you know how awful it was to be left here, not knowing when, or even if, you'd come back for me? We're supposed to be partners. I'm in training. Care to explain to me how I can be trained when I don't know what the hell is going on?"

Were her eyes playing tricks on her or did his grin just widen? "Don't just stand there, you moron. Say something!"

"God, I missed you."

"I don't care— What?" That wasn't the answer she expected. She paused in the midst of her finger-poking-in-the-chest tirade, her mouth hung open in surprise.

"I missed you like crazy. You're like a damn drug in my system, Nevada, and I can't get you out."

Oh that was a cheap shot. And so unfair. She scrambled to find the right retort, but only managed, "I...you...we..."

"My thoughts exactly." He pulled her roughly against him and swept his mouth over hers in a blindsiding kiss.

Chapter Ten

All the careful control she'd planned over her life shot out the open window of Tyler's bedroom. The second his lips met hers, she couldn't come up with a single coherent thought, nor could she protest his unconventional way of ending their argument.

Maybe it was the anger she'd held barely in check during the day and a half he'd been gone. Then again, maybe it was the fact that this is what she'd needed and wanted all along, what she'd craved from the first moment his deep, toe-curling masculine voice made her thankful to be a woman. His mouth on her, his hands roaming over her back and shoulders. He pulled her closer until her aching sex pressed intimately against his hard cock.

They still had a lot to settle between them, the least of which was his drop and run escapade yesterday. But she was tired of fighting the passion between them. Everything else could wait. Right now she needed *this* more than anything.

She clasped her arms around his waist, daring to trail her hands down to his buttocks. She rocked against his erection, desperately wishing their clothes would disappear. More than anything she wanted him inside her, part of her, as she'd dreamed about for so many lonely nights.

"I don't know where to kiss you first, where to touch you." His voice rasped in her ear, quick and harsh. She thrilled at his passionate frustration.

She tilted her head back, allowing him access to her neck. He ravaged her like a thirsty vampire, scraping his teeth over the side of her neck, pressing kisses and light nips against her throat until she moaned out loud.

He covered her moans with his lips, drawing her tongue inside his mouth, sucking lightly. She tangled her tongue with his, a lover's dance of heat that was but a promise of what would come later.

He backed her up—each kiss, each caress moving them toward the bed. She felt the edge of the mattress against the back of her knees and suddenly she was falling.

"I've got you, don't worry," he whispered as his hands gently lowered her to the bed. He bent forward, his face looming over hers. Not quite touching her, she felt the draw of his heat.

"Please," she whispered back, unable to tell him exactly what she wanted. All she knew was their bodies weren't touching intimately and she craved his warmth as if it were bitter January, not sultry July.

His smile told her he'd gotten the idea. He settled his body over hers, a perfect fit. Her heat against his, her softness against his pulsating hardness. She wrapped her legs around him, ran her fingers through his thick, dark hair and pulled his mouth to hers.

"You make me forget everything but you." He murmured against her lips and slid his hands underneath to cup her buttocks, surging against her until she bit lightly against his lip to keep from crying out. They rolled over the bed, once, twice, until he bumped a lamp with his foot, sending it crashing to the floor.

They bolted upright. She was certain one or both of Tyler's parents would come running down the hall any second. The noise was a definite mood breaker. They sat on the edge of the bed, trying to catch their breath and waiting to be discovered.

Nothing. He sighed, threw out a vicious curse and ran his hands through his hair.

"What's wrong?"

His passion glazed eyes fixed on her. "This isn't going to work," he said in a low voice.

Seemed to be working just fine for her. "What's not going to work?"

He swept his hand over his room. "This. Here. With my parents down the hall. Dammit, I feel like a sixteen-year-old again, trying not to get caught while I make it with one of my classmates in the garage."

"The way I heard it, it wasn't a classmate, it was a neighbor in her early twenties. And you did get caught."

"I can't believe my mother told you that story."

At his look of shocked horror, she lifted an eyebrow and grinned. "Your mother told me a lot of stories." She pursed her lips together to keep from laughing.

"What kind of stories?"

"All kinds. From sucking your thumb until you were six, to getting caught with the blonde nympho from down the street."

He shook his head. "Damn. I knew I shouldn't have left you alone with her. That's why I never brought women over. She blabs about everything in my past."

This time she did laugh. "It's not her fault you, um, misbehaved when you were younger."

His eyes half-closed, he bent his head toward her, grasping her waist and pulling her on top of him. "Misbehaved, did I?" He moved, lifting his hips against her. "Is this misbehaving?"

She shuddered at the feel of his hard shaft against her pussy. "Oh yes."

"And do you disapprove?"

Breathing deeply as his hands roamed over her back and buttocks, she shook her head. "Absolutely not."

"Want more?"

"Yes."

"How much more?"

The way his hands evoked her body's response should be outlawed. It simply wasn't fair. "Everything. I want everything."

"Now?"

She lost herself in the darkening depths of his eyes. "No. Next month. Of course, now."

His body shuddered against her. "Let's go." Gently, he pushed her off and went to the closet, grabbing a blanket.

"Go where?"

He grasped her hand and pulled her to her feet. "Someplace where we can do what we want, be as loud as we want, without having to worry about waking my parents."

A good plan. It didn't matter if they went to the backseat of his car. At this point she'd follow him anywhere.

He led her downstairs and quietly opened the back door, leading out to the covered veranda. The scent of roses filled the air. She remembered seeing the red climbers earlier in the day, skirting their way through the open lattice of the porch.

The path led past landscaped gardens, tall trees and perfectly trimmed bushes, providing a privacy wall for the pool area.

It was magnificent, lit up by the moonlit sky. Deathly still, not a single ripple marred the glass-like surface of the Olympic-sized pool. Here, fragrant gardenias climbed the walls of the surrounding white lattice, their scent bringing to mind tropical nights. The humidity and water only added to the illusion.

The pool house was small, no bigger than a three-car garage. It was bright and airy, double windows on either side of the door providing a visual of the pool. An oversized white wicker chaise sat against the inner wall, its plump lavender cushion inviting and roomy enough for two people.

"Want a drink?" Tyler threw the blanket on the chaise and turned to the wet bar.

"Yes, I'd love one. Whatever you're having is fine."

"I'm having a beer."

Just what she needed to quench her thirst. At least one of her thirsts. Her eyes followed him like a desert flower searching out the single drop of rain that sustains its life.

"Let's sit down," he said, motioning her to the chaise. He leaned back against the cushions and pulled her down between his outstretched legs, her back against his chest.

It seemed almost awkward now, sitting with him and quietly sipping a drink. After their heated argument and rushed frenzy of passion, followed by relocating, how were they going to get back to where they were before?

Did she even want to? Had she foolishly gotten caught up in their kiss, only to act recklessly without considering the ramifications of her actions?

"What are you thinking about?" His question, whispered against her neck, made her shiver. "Nothing."

"Liar." His laugh vibrated against her back. "You were thinking about what we were doing earlier, weren't you?"

Did she have a mirror in the back of her head? How could he so easily read her thoughts? "Maybe."

"Second thoughts?"

Damn if he didn't do it again. "Maybe."

"Still want me?"

Definitely. "Maybe."

She waited for his next question, but he went silent. She shifted to search his face, his silence unnerving her. Maybe he was having second thoughts now. Finally, she couldn't stand it. "And you?"

"What about me?"

"Are *you* having second thoughts?" After all, they'd started and stopped so many times she was beginning to wonder if he really wanted her at all.

His sensuous smile devastated her. "Hell, no. I don't have second thoughts. I want you, Nevada."

His words slid right into her heart. He wanted her, wanted to make love to her. And she wanted him too, more than just physically. She wanted to crawl inside his heart and set up permanent residence.

In past relationships, this was the point where she usually begged off, ended whatever might happen. This was the road she usually didn't take. Whenever emotions took over, she went running.

But not with Tyler.

Her feelings for him were escalating, turning into more than just simple fantasy and attraction. Part of her was scared to death. The other part was simply tired of fighting against love. What would happen if she opened her heart and let love inside?

His face held no expectation, only interest. He'd put the ball in her court, letting her decide what happened next. Any hesitation she may have felt disappeared. She wanted this. As for what would happen afterward, she'd deal with it later.

She turned halfway to lean against him, her eyes making contact with his. "Make love to me, Tyler."

His fingers trailed against her cheek before sliding behind her neck, pulling her face toward his. "About damn time."

This time his kiss wasn't gentle. It was demanding, physical and loaded with passion.

Never before had she felt so wanted, so desired. Tyler's heart pounded against her breast. She was lightheaded, like she'd been running for hours and couldn't take in enough oxygen to fuel her starving brain. Everything seemed surreal, including this moment, with this man.

His lips performed magic, weaving a spell over her senses until all she could focus on were the sensations of his mouth. She caressed the side of his face, feeling the scratch of his unshaven jaw against the sensitive skin of her palm. Lightning-like tingles shot straight between her legs.

He pulled his mouth away from her. "You keep making those sounds and I'm going to go through the roof in record time."

"Sounds?"

"Yeah. Moans and little whimpers in the back of your throat. Drives me crazy."

She liked the thought of driving him crazy. She tried to do it consciously, but he only laughed at her.

"You can't force it. It comes naturally when you kiss me."

"Let's see if we can replicate it naturally, then." A quick shift on the chaise and she was in his lap, facing him, her legs locked behind his back. Sliding her hands once more to his face, she leaned in and pressed her mouth against his.

Such soft, full lips for such a tough guy. So damn sexy she whimpered for what only he could give her.

"There it is again," he murmured against her lips.

She gasped as his hands slid up her rib cage, under her shirt. Her stomach jumped at his touch. Their eyes met, locked on each other as he continued his exploration of her skin.

The shirt bunched under his hands as he pushed it up toward her breasts, his thumbs lightly scraping her already sensitized skin. She lifted her arms and he pulled the shirt over her head, baring her breasts to his gaze.

His lips brushed her hair, his hands continuing their exploration of her breasts. "You have the softest skin. And you smell like vanilla. God, I love that." The contact of his fingers on her nipples was electric, shocking them into hardened nubs at his slightest touch.

As if the feel of his hands weren't enough to make her mad, he leaned forward and lightly fit his mouth over one distended nipple.

She arched her back as if she could somehow fit more into his greedy mouth. He circled her nipple, sucking it gently between his lips, his teeth lightly scraping against her. Instinctively she pushed her hips against him, needing to assuage the nonstop agony his touch created.

He laid her against the cushions and leaned over her, his midnight eyes black as a moonless night. Then he bent down and swirled his tongue over each upraised nipple, once and then again, until she threaded her fingers through his hair and pulled his head toward her face, desperate for the contact of his mouth against hers.

Relentlessly, he continued his assault. He kissed her long and thoroughly, at the same time unbuttoning her shorts. With one highly skilled hand he pulled them over her hips, using his feet to push them off.

She was completely bare except for her panties, while he was still fully clothed. That wouldn't do at all.

"I want you naked, too," she said in a raspy voice that didn't sound like her own.

His half-hooded eyes opened wide along with his smile. "Then, undress me."

Returning his smile, she sat up and grabbed at his shirt, pulling it over his head. Without hesitation she wound her fingers through the crisp hair spattered across his chest, seeking and finding his sensitive nipples. She trailed her fingers around them, satisfied when they beaded under her touch.

There was so much about his body she wanted to explore and yet she was torn between taking the time to learn every inch of him and the desire to rip his clothes off.

Time enough for slow exploration later. She wanted him naked, now. The zipper on his jeans gave way easily. Without bothering to slide his pants down she dipped her hand inside, reaching for his hot, throbbing cock. He groaned and thrust against her palm. She pushed his jeans partway down and pulled his shaft free of his boxers.

Finally, she touched and stroked the part of him she'd been desperate to for over a week. Thick and hard, it pulsed against her hand as she drew her palm from the base of his shaft to the tip. Drops of silken liquid spilled over the top of his cock and she swiped it away with her thumb, circling the sensitive head.

Hissing out a ragged curse, Tyler grasped her wrist and pulled her hand away, gently pressing against her shoulder to lay her down.

"I've thought about this a hundred times. Every time I heard your voice on the phone, whispering to me in a way I'd want you to if I had you naked underneath me."

Heart slamming against her chest, she watched with a mixture of curiosity and appreciation as he stood before her and slid his jeans, then his boxers, completely off.

He took her breath away, his body all chiseled angles and planes. Tanned, well-muscled in all the right places, but not too much. His body could grace the cover of any magazine. Broad shoulders, lean hips and a cock that made her lick her lips in anticipation. Before she could sit up he crawled onto the chaise beside her, stroking her hip as they faced each other.

"You have a magnificent body," he murmured as his lips took hers in a soul-shattering kiss. "I want to kiss and explore every part of it, but not now. Now I need to be inside you more than I need to breathe."

Her pussy wept its response, her hips flexing against him like a magnet in search of steel. He turned her onto her back again, grasping her panties and sliding them down her legs.

Despite his comment about moving things along quickly, he stilled, staring at her, his gaze traveling over her body in a way that should have made her feel self-conscious, but didn't. He touched her, beginning at her thigh and moving up her hip, his fingers drawing lazy circles in random patterns on her skin. She grasped his shoulders, moaning long and low as he sought and found the slickened slit that begged for him.

"You're so wet, so ready for me."

She couldn't respond. Her voice caught on a sobbing gasp as he dipped a finger inside her, moving lazily in a rhythmic dance. His thumb traced a circle around her clit and she tightened around his finger, pulses of pleasure lifting her hips in invitation. A prelude, a tease of what was to come.

It was unbearable, this intense mixture of joy and pain. "Tyler, please." Unable to stand his tender assault, she ran her hands over his chest and stomach, then lower, trailing her fingers over his shaft. She grasped it, stroking it slowly, matching the rhythm of his finger thrusting inside her.

It had been so long since she'd felt the joy of a man's body against hers. No, that wasn't right. Somewhere in her pleasure-soaked brain she knew it had never been like this before.

They stayed that way for what seemed like an eternity, stroking and kissing, exploring and learning, until with a low growl he moved over her, nudging her legs apart with his knee and settling himself between them, his erection caressing her aching cunt.

He poised, searching her face with a look so tender it brought a tear rolling from the corner of her eye. He bent and licked the tear from her cheek at the same time he slid inside her.

Had she ever really made love before this? She'd always kept a part of herself remote, distancing the act from the feelings. But then again, the few men she'd been with before hadn't captured her heart, her very soul, like this one did.

A part of her knew the risk of allowing him entry into a place no one had been before—the locked recesses of her tender heart. But she could no more deny him than she could deny her body the sustenance it needed for life.

They rocked together, lost in a pool of sensations as he stroked within her, slow at first and then gathering speed as their desire increased. She raised her hips to meet his as he thrust harder each time.

Every one of her senses was alive and tuned in to only him. His rasping breath and moans of encouragement took her ever higher. The scent of him filled her, that musky, male scent an aphrodisiac no cologne could ever duplicate. Her eyes drank him in, every passion-filled look drawing her deeper inside that private part of him she knew not many had ever seen. His touch evoked everything female about her to her weep with joy.

"Your pussy is hot and tight," he said, his jaw clenched and his eyes so dark she was lost in them. "God I love the way you squeeze my cock."

His voice, as always, drove her to the brink of rapturous insanity.

It was unbearable, this race to find a pinnacle she so desperately craved. All coherent thought scattered as she climbed with him, stroke by stroke, her body heated with every caress, every uttered word. He kissed her, whispered to her, touched her, all the while driving deeply within her until the end she so desperately searched for was within her grasp.

"Look at me, Nevada. Come with me, now."

As if she had a choice in the matter. His pelvis ground against her clit, a spiraling, intense sensation that sent her pussy into spasms.

"Now, Tyler!" she cried, then opened her eyes and locked on his face as her orgasm took her deep within him. He groaned and stilled as he climaxed along with her, taking her mouth in a kiss that bound her soul to his.

They tumbled together, his hands holding tight to her buttocks as he plunged deep, pouring into her waiting pussy, sending her spiraling toward another climax just as intense as the first. She cried out and dug her nails into his back, never wanting to separate, never wanting the exquisite sensations to stop.

The ebb took awhile, tiny pulses continuing to ping inside her. Tyler's muscles relaxed and he pulled her to his side, still joined as he kissed her hair and face until she closed her eyes, more content than she'd ever been in her life.

It wasn't until sometime later she woke, taking a few minutes to gather her bearings. They'd fallen asleep, lying on the chaise, their bodies entwined. Tyler had somehow turned them around so he was on his back, her head resting on his chest.

Had she ever felt so content, so complete? She inhaled a quaking breath, overcome with what they'd experienced together.

Had it been the same way for him? A life-altering, emotional exchange of heart and soul? Or had she just imagined the intensity on his face, the more-than-just-sex caresses of his hands over her body?

Chancing a glance at Tyler, her heart stirred at the sight of his slumbering face. His long, dark lashes rested against his cheekbone, the dark stubble along his jaw making him look reckless and dangerous.

She swept her fingers along his hair, brushing it back from his forehead. He was such a contradiction. Both dangerous and the safest thing in her life. In sleep he looked vulnerable, innocent. She was stunned by the realization that sent her from drowsy to fully awake.

What she had feared all along had happened. What she had tried to control for so many years had become uncontrollable.

As if her life hadn't changed enough in the past week, this had to happen too. Her fantasy man had come to full-blown life and stolen her carefully guarded heart right out from under its protective shield.

She'd fallen in love with Tyler Call.

Chapter Eleven

࿇

Tyler let out a resigned sigh. Making love with Nevada had changed everything. Not that it all hadn't changed before that.

Now he had decisions to make. Big, life-altering ones. First, what to do about his job, now that he really saw things clearly. Second, what to do about the fact that he'd fallen in love with Nevada.

He examined maps in the living room while she worked in the office on the laptop. After returning to the condo a few days ago, they'd settled into a cozy routine. Sleeping in, making love throughout the day and working on the mission. Then making love again at night, sometimes all night long.

All the years he'd spent trying to become a hero like his father, he'd overlooked the one heroic thing he could have done.

Giving his heart and allowing himself to love.

He glanced across the room at her. She worked steadily, frowning and chewing her bottom lip.

"Find anything?"

"Not now." She brushed him off with a wave of her hand, her eyes never once leaving the monitor.

She also got cranky if he interrupted her research.

So he stayed quiet and watched her, feeling a contentment that had always eluded him. Gone was the restlessness that had dominated his life for the past fifteen years. Ever since high school, he'd had goals. Big goals, about military service and covert operations and doing something monumental.

Well, he'd finally managed the monumental. He'd fallen in love.

And now he had to change his life. But first he had to keep them both alive and in order to do that he needed to finish the mission. Get the cartel off his and Nevada's trail. Then he'd find out who was the insider at the Agency.

At the same time, he had to protect her. She'd become more than just an assignment. She was precious to him and he had to make sure no harm came to her.

No small goals. But necessary. He couldn't begin his future life without completing the tasks in the present.

Enough of this. He stood and walked into the office, stopping behind Nevada.

Did she even know he was there? He bent down and pressed a light kiss against the back of her neck, expecting her to jump and yell at him for destroying her concentration.

Instead she made a purring sound, scrunching her shoulders and offering a rippling, deep-throated laugh that reverberated through him. Raging desire arced inside him, hardening him instantly.

"That felt nice. Do it again."

"My pleasure." This time he nipped lightly at the back of her neck. She shivered and leaned back in the chair, stretching her arms over her head. She wore only his T-shirt and he took a moment to admire her breasts pressed against the thin cotton. And her legs, peeking out under the shirt— now those were a work of art.

She tilted her head all the way back, looking at him upside down. "You keep that up and we won't get very far in our research."

"That's not fair. I want you."

"Oh, but you want the location of the drug cartel's incoming shipment more, don't you?"

"That's a loaded question, kind of like the one women always ask."

"What question women ask?"

He grinned. "The one about whether or not their clothes make them look fat. There is no right answer."

"Take a shot," she said, her eyes crossing as she smirked at him.

He pressed a kiss against her upside down lips. "Not a chance, partner. I know better. Back to work for you." Reluctantly, he stepped away and took his place back on the couch and watched her.

What he really wanted to do was gather her into his arms and make love to her right there, on the floor of the office. He was hard and ready and all she'd done was kiss him.

Every day they spent together he grew more and more concerned that his mind was no longer on the mission. And that could have devastating results for both of them. His inattention to completing the assignment put her at risk. Before, he'd never had to worry about anyone but himself. That was no longer true.

But what could he do? Taking her to his parents had been somewhat risky, except his father had the property wired up with extremely sophisticated technology. One didn't get to be a Marine General and the Commander of the NCA without making a few enemies along the way. It wasn't obvious to the naked eye but there was plenty of protection at his father's home.

Maybe he should just drop her off and focus his attention on the meth lab shipments. Once he brought in the key players, he and Nevada would be free to do whatever they wanted. Until then, he couldn't concentrate on his work and worry about her at the same time.

"Hey! I found something!"

"What is it?" He headed over and stepped behind her, looking over her shoulder.

"It may be nothing, but there's an expected shipment coming in from Mercado International next week."

He followed the information on the screen. "It could be a legit shipment."

"True. But it could also be exactly what you're looking for. Here's why. See how most of their shipments are of textiles?"

"Yeah."

"The one coming in next week is flour and bakery equipment, scheduled for delivery to some obscure warehouse."

"Go on."

"I scanned their bills of lading for the past six months. There've been three incoming deliveries of flour and bakery equipment, out of a total of twenty-four shipments."

He straightened and looked at her. "And we know of at least three incidents of distribution of chemicals and meth supplies in the past six months."

She nodded and smiled. "Exactly."

"You may be on to something. Where's the shipment being delivered?"

"On the other side of the river. A complex of warehouses in East St. Louis."

"Which is a perfect cover. I know the area. Hundreds of trucks go in and out every day making deliveries."

"Do you think this is it?"

"Might be. I'll check it out." He kissed the top of her head. "Good job, partner."

She beamed a grin.

They printed the data and sat on the couch together, reviewing the past history of shipments and deliveries.

"All three previous flour and bakery equipment deliveries had been taken to different warehouses. That doesn't make sense."

One of the things he found so attractive about her was her analytical mind. "You're right. I'm convinced this is the shipment we've been looking for."

Her eyes shone with excitement. "And it's coming in less than a week. So now what?"

"I don't have many options." He ran his fingers through a silken strand of her dark hair. "If I could trust the NCA, we'd be making arrangements for a bust. As it is, I have no one to rely on but myself."

She straightened, leveling her gaze at him. "Excuse me, but you *do* have someone to rely on. I'm here, I'm supposed to be in training and I can help."

He didn't like the direction this conversation was going. "You *have* helped. Your research skills are phenomenal." He laughed and kissed her. "But you're not a field agent."

She leaned back and crossed her arms. "Not a field agent *yet*. You're supposed to be training me, remember?"

He tried to keep his grin at bay. "I know that, but this also isn't the best venue for training, since your life is also at risk right now and we don't know who to trust. Besides, you're an analyst, Nevada, and a damn good one at that." At least she managed a slightly pleased smile at that one. "But you don't even know how to use a gun."

She tilted toward him and grasped his hands. "I do too. I've had weapons training."

"Training on the firing range isn't the same thing as trying to defend yourself while on the run."

"Then teach me. I'm not incompetent, Tyler. If I were, they'd never have selected me for the training program. Let me help. You can't do this by yourself."

"Absolutely not. I'm supposed to be protecting you, remember? Not putting you in the line of fire."

"But—"

"No."

She stood, pacing in front of the couch. "I'm trained by NCA. Granted, I haven't had any field training, but I can go along as lookout for you."

"Nevada, you can't—"

Hands on hips, she glared at him. "Don't tell me I can't. I can and you don't have one good damn reason why I can't."

He didn't answer her, didn't know what to say. He wasn't going to put her at risk.

She kneeled in front of him, her eyes filled with concern. "Tyler, please. Everyone I've ever cared about has died and I could do nothing to control it. Don't leave me sitting here worrying about you when I could be out there helping you. I can wield a weapon, maybe not as good as you or Legend, but well enough to hit a target."

He sighed, knowing she'd beat this subject to death.

No way in hell would he ever put her in that kind of danger. But he also understood her desire to help and didn't want to spend the next five days arguing with her about it. Nor would he let her know what his real plan was. When the time came, he'd make sure she was safe and nowhere near the warehouse. If she got pissed about that, so be it. He'd rather risk her ire than her life.

But for now, a little placating was in order.

"Okay, we'll work on some weapons training."

She grinned. "Great! When?"

He looked at his watch. "Later tonight. Let's go out and get something to eat. I know someone who owns a firing range. A close friend from my military days. I trust him completely. He'll let us in after the range closes for the night."

She nodded and jumped up to shower and change for dinner. Tyler breathed a sigh of relief. He'd gotten a reprieve. She was going to be angry as hell when she found out what he was planning. But that was several days away. For now, he'd enjoy the time they had together and hope it wasn't going to be their last.

* * * * *

"Dave King and I go way back," Tyler explained as he pulled into the driveway of King's Gun Range. "We were in boot camp together and did recon training at the same time."

Nevada nodded, nervously chewing her lip. She'd had basic weapons training, but hadn't handled a gun in a very long time. What she hadn't told Tyler was that it was doubtful she could even remember how to load one, let alone fire it.

Nevertheless, she'd demanded the lesson. Like it or not, she was going to get it. Besides, she could at least hold a gun on someone until they figured out what to do. But she was not going to let Tyler go out there alone, without any backup.

"He gave me his security code and said he'd leave the key behind the mailbox. Here it is." Tyler withdrew a key from behind the silver mailbox affixed to the brick wall next to the front door. He slipped it in the lock and stepped inside, punching in the codes to deactivate the security alarm.

"Hold my hand," he said as they entered the pitch-black lobby. "I'm not going to turn lights on until we're on the range."

After he closed and locked the front door she was completely blind. But Tyler's night vision was useful once again. He shifted her this way and that as if he knew the way.

A light flipped on and they were bathed in brightness.

She blinked and surveyed the huge firing range. A series of private cubicles were lined up side by side. Other than that, there was nothing but an empty stretch of flooring between the countertop of the cubicle and the human-shaped paper target at the other end of the range.

"We'll start simple," he said, grabbing a gun out of the waistband of his jeans. "I'll explain how it works and get you comfortable with it before we do any firing."

She nodded, hoping she paid close enough attention so she wouldn't shoot herself, literally, in the foot.

The pistol was a nine millimeter automatic. At least she knew the basics about that model.

"What's the difference between a nine millimeter and a ten millimeter?" She laughed at his horrified look. "I was joking."

He shook his head and released the clip from the gun, jacking the round out of the chamber. "Okay, take it."

She inspected it closely as he explained the features, paying close attention to the location of the safety mechanism and how it worked. He walked her through loading the clip and working the slide action to cock it.

When he was confident she felt at ease with a loaded weapon in her hand, he instructed her on preparing to fire it. They put on their safety glasses and ear protection and stepped into the cubicle.

"Turn toward the target first. Always make sure the gun is cocked and the safety is off."

"It's hard to cock this thing," she said, awkwardly attempting to slide the mechanism back.

"Like this," he said and put his hand over hers, effortlessly easing the slide back until it clicked into place. "It's not that hard, just awkward when you're not used to it."

She inhaled deeply. "It's been awhile since I've fired a weapon. Give me a minute here and I'll be blowing their heads off."

He laughed. "Now, raise your arms and hold it the way I showed you. Take a stance like you're going to fire."

She spread her legs apart and held her arms up, but straightened her elbows.

"Not that way. When you lock up like that, your body will shake and you won't be able to hit anything." He reached up and wrapped his hands around her forearms, pulling her arms back and bending her elbows. "Like this. It's more relaxed and will make your aim better."

She smelled good. He buried his nose in her hair and leaned closer, settling in against her backside. He fervently hoped this wouldn't be a lengthy lesson. He was getting hotter by the minute, his mind occupied with thoughts of sliding his hands up that short, sexy skirt she wore, instead of focusing on her shooting.

"Okay, I'm ready," she said.

So was he. Ignoring the erection trying to take away his concentration, he positioned himself firmly behind her. "Get ready for the kick, like I told you, and relax. Keep in mind you don't want to aim for the head. Go for the midsection—it's a larger target area."

She nodded, took a deep breath and pulled the trigger. And missed the target completely.

"Where did I hit it?"

"About five feet above his head."

"Oh shit. That's not good."

"It's okay. Actually, not bad for your first try." Her perfume snuck into his senses—that natural woman scent mixed with a subtle sprinkling of vanilla. It was a powerfully erotic potion, adding to his awareness of her body pressed intimately against his.

"Can we do it again?"

"Sure. This time," he whispered against her ear, "keep your eyes open."

She giggled and set her legs apart.

"Now, position your body this way," he said, his voice lower than it should be. Grasping her hips, he moved her gently against him, unable to resist the soft, lush feel of her body.

"Um, this way?" She pressed her ass back against him while placing her arms in position.

He bit back a groan. "Yeah, like that." Definitely like that. Sliding his arms over hers, he grasped her elbows and pulled them back, lightly scraping the sides of her breasts with his fingers.

"Is this the right way?" Once again, she bent forward enough to tilt her buttocks against his hard-on.

"I think you've got it just right," he said harshly, all but panting behind her. Sweat formed on his face and neck as he held tight to her hips, loving the feel of her rhythmic rocking against him.

They stayed like that a few minutes, gently swaying, until they both forgot completely about the firing lesson. Nevada dropped the clip out of the gun and laid the weapon on the countertop in front of her. She pulled off the glasses and ear protection, then leaned forward against the counter, pushing her bottom against his rock-hard length.

"Is there another lesson you want?" he asked, taking off his protective gear and tossing them behind him.

"As a matter of fact there is." She moaned when he found her breasts.

In answer to her silent pleas, he cupped the soft mounds, sliding his fingers over her nipples. "I can see you need some serious one-on-one tutoring." He pressed harder against her, trailing one hand down her waist and over her hip to the hem of her skirt. He raised the skirt and slid his hand underneath, shocked and rocketed with desire to discover she wore no panties.

"Damn, woman, that's hot as hell." He probed between her legs, searching for that spot he craved to touch. When he found her slit he petted her pussy lips, drawing the wetness there and using it to caress her swollen clit. She gasped and he moved down again, circling her cunt, poised to enter her, but wanting to tease her for a few seconds.

"Please." Her begging whisper made his balls draw tight against his body. But he wanted to take his time, despite his cock's urging to lift her skirt and plunge hard and fast inside her wet pussy.

"I know what you want, baby." And he would be the only man to ever give it to her.

"Tyler," she cried when he slipped his fingers inside her. She was moist and hot as boiling water. Her head thrown back against his shoulder, she whimpered when he withdrew his fingers to caress her clit again.

She reached behind and cupped him through the denim. He swore out a frustrated curse at the jeans that separated her hand from his aching flesh, and savagely tore the zipper down, allowing her access inside.

He bit back a groan as she twined her fingers around his shaft, sliding her hand firmly along his length until his aching need for her overruled any semblance of reason.

Pushing her forward against the counter, he took a half step back, slid his jeans down and raised her skirt over her hips. He probed her slick entrance and plunged inside.

She cried out and threw her head back against his shoulder. He leaned into her embrace, turning her face to the side with his hand so he could take her mouth with the same desperate intensity as their coupling.

He focused on her ass as she bucked back to meet his thrusts, the perfect globes moving in unison with his strokes. He longed to slip between those cheeks and sink inside her tight rosette, but was loathe to pull out of the hot sheath of her pussy. He dipped his fingers between them and drew her juices onto his hand, then teased her anal entrance with light strokes, slipping just enough inside that she whimpered and moved backward, trying to impale her ass onto his finger.

"Someday I'm going to fuck your ass," he said through clenched teeth, fighting the need to shoot inside her right now. First he wanted to hear the cries of her climax, and, when the muscles of her cunt squeezed around his straining cock, he'd come in her.

His balls hardened as he readied for release. Reaching in front of them, he found her clit and stroked furiously. Nevada threw her head back and screamed as her orgasm hit, its echo bouncing off the walls of the deserted range.

Her passionate cries fueled his own intense need to release until he could hold back no longer, his low growl intensifying into a roar of pleasure as he held tight to her hips and thrust hard once more, then emptied his cum inside her.

He collapsed over her, their sweat-soaked clothes sticking together.

Nothing like this had ever happened to him before. He'd never lost control like that, never felt such a fierce need to be with a woman. He pulled her hair aside and pressed a kiss against her neck. She purred her contentment at him.

"Are you okay?"

She nodded and turned to face him, a satisfied smirk on her face. "Definitely."

They looked at each other; clothes disheveled like a couple of backseat teenagers, and broke out into fits of laughter.

"Interesting training," she finally managed as they righted their clothing.

Tyler handed her a soft drink he'd purchased from the machine right outside the range. "I can give you as many lessons like that as you'd like."

She sipped the drink, stopping only to press the cold can between her breasts. Tyler felt his blood begin to race again as she handed him the can and he placed it on the counter.

"Does that mean our instruction for the night is over?" she asked, one brow arched wickedly, a gleam in her cat-like eyes.

"Oh no, I have a lot more to teach you."

She stepped into his arms. "Bring it on," she said, pulling him into a passionate kiss.

Chapter Twelve

సిం

They'd slept most of the morning away. Tyler didn't care, knowing there wasn't much more to do before tonight. Before he even opened his eyes he smiled. A warm body rested next to his, her even breathing indicating she wasn't disturbed by his restless state.

He kissed the top of Nevada's head and eased his arm out from underneath her. She mumbled and rolled over onto her stomach, clutching the pillow against her.

That was *his* woman lying there asleep, her hair rumpled from their wild romp under the covers last night. She amazed him with her open sensuality. Every wanton suggestion he made to tease and shock her was greeted with curiosity and enthusiasm. Never before had he met a woman to match his desires. Until now.

With great reluctance he tore his gaze away, slipped on his shorts and headed into the kitchen to make coffee.

Time to think. The shipment was due in at nine tonight by barge, which would put the trucks at the warehouse by ten-thirty or so. He made mental notes of positioning based upon the advance reconnaissance he and Nevada had done a couple days ago. They'd driven past the row of warehouses, pinpointing the exact location where the shipment would be delivered.

Now he had it set in his mind. If the major players showed up, it would be a winning bust all around. There was always the possibility the CEO of Mercado wouldn't be on hand tonight. But this being their biggest shipment, he had a hunch the big guns would make an appearance to insure their merchandise was distributed correctly. They had a lot to lose if anything went wrong.

Tyler would make sure they lost it all. The only problem was, how would he manage the mission by himself?

"Morning, partner."

He turned and regarded Nevada's barefoot progress into the kitchen. "Afternoon, you mean." He kissed her on the mouth, then directed her to the kitchen chair. She plopped in it and laid her head in her folded arms.

"What time did we go to sleep last night?" she mumbled with a wide yawn.

"We slept?"

She opened one eye and grinned at him. "A couple hours, maybe."

"You complaining?" He placed a steaming cup of coffee next to her and sat down.

"No way." Finally she raised her head and took a sip of the steaming brew. "What time do we leave for the warehouse tonight?"

This was the part he hated. Lying to her. "About seven."

She frowned at him. "Why so early? I thought the shipment wasn't due at the warehouse until ten-thirty?"

"I want to stop by my dad's house first."

"Oh? Why?"

He shrugged. "Just a couple things I want to get straight in my mind about the mission, and I wanted to ask his opinion."

"Okay. It'll be nice to see your mother again."

"You two really hit it off, didn't you?"

She nodded and graced him with a sleepy smile. "Yes, we did. I like your mother very much, Tyler. She's a wonderful woman."

Reaching up to smooth a flyaway hair from her face, he leaned in for a kiss. "She likes you, too." He touched his forehead against hers, unable to get enough of her skin and her scent.

They ate, then discussed the plan until very late in the afternoon. Tyler began to pack his duffle bag for the evening's activities.

Nevada had never seen an armory like the one he was sliding into the compact bags. It was frightening to think of him using any of those vicious-looking assault weapons, but she vowed to back him up no matter what.

Even if the only thing she knew how to use was a handgun. She'd defend him with her life if necessary.

They'd gone to the firing range two more times after that first night, but actually managed to stick to the shooting lessons. She warmed remembering that first night, the overwhelming passion whenever they were together. It was like two combustible substances that, once touched, exploded in a fiery burst of light and heat.

She'd never felt this way before, never allowed a man to get close enough to capture her heart. Until Tyler. It frightened and thrilled her at the same time. What would happen after all this was over, she didn't know. And now wasn't the time to think about it.

Right now her goal was to help him stay alive. Then they'd figure out the rest.

"You're putting grenades in there?"

"Yeah. I might need an explosion for a diversion."

She shuddered, a feeling of dread pressing closer as the day wore on. Now that the moment was upon them, the realization of what Tyler was going to try to do alone frightened her more than it ever had.

The risks he took could get him killed. He'd be outnumbered for certain. Despite the fact he told her she was getting better on the firing range, she knew she'd be of no help to him at all should the situation get out of hand.

Surely there had to be someone at the agency they could trust. Someone who could help. But who?

"You ready?" He zipped the last of the bags and stood.

He looked like a commando, dressed in all-black clothing and military issue boots.

"Shouldn't I dress the same way?"

"Not necessary. You've got jeans and a dark shirt. That'll do. I don't expect you to have to follow inches behind me anyway. I want you out of sight and out of danger, unless I need you."

"That's not quite the backup I had in mind."

He half-smiled. "Remember, I'm your training officer. You're supposed to follow my orders. When I train a new recruit it's also my responsibility to keep them out of danger."

She wanted to argue about that, but knew he was right. Charging gung ho in there and having Tyler worrying about her safety wouldn't do him any good. "I'll follow your orders."

Finally, they were ready. She picked up her bag and prepared to leave, but Tyler's hand on her arm stopped her. She turned to him.

"Before we leave, I need to say something to you." He lifted the strap of her bag and placed it on the floor, then pulled her against him, winding his arms tightly around her.

She laid her head on his shoulder, feeling safe and secure in his embrace. Then she pulled away. "What is it?"

A worried look filled his eyes. But she also saw something she'd seen only recently. A warmth, like a distant flame in the darkness—a beacon to the lost. "When this is over, we need to talk."

"About what?"

"About you and me," he said solemnly, pressing a light kiss against her lips.

"What about you and me?"

"About our future and what happens with us after this mission ends."

Her stomach did flip-flops. Did that mean an ending, or a beginning? She was almost too afraid to ask, and equally as afraid of what his answer would be. Living in the here and now the past couple weeks had been perfect. An idyllic fantasy come to life. But the reality of their relationship would be different. When this was over, she had some thinking to do.

"I want to make some changes in my life. Some of those changes involve you."

There was an indicator of the direction of his thoughts. Her heart jumped a little, and comforting warmth spread over her. He cared for her, that much was certain. But how much, and in what way?

She opened her mouth to ask, but he placed his finger on her lips. "Not now. We don't have time to get into it. But we will," he said, following up his light kiss with one deeper, one full of longing and promise, one she returned with just as much promise.

If he wanted her in his life after this, they had much to talk about. But not now.

* * * * *

By the time they arrived at his parents' house, it was near dark. Margaret greeted them with a wide grin.

"I'm so happy to see you!" She threw her arms around Nevada and hugged her tight, then kissed Tyler on the cheek. "What are you doing here?"

They stepped inside and Margaret shut the door. Nevada clutched her personal bag of weaponry close, feeling a bit awkward about carrying all this firepower into Tyler's parents' house.

"I just needed to talk to Dad for a minute. Is he around?"

"In the family room watching the baseball game," she said.

Tyler nodded and started down the hall.

"Come in and visit with me while I start dinner," Margaret said, pulling Nevada along.

She really wanted to go with Tyler, hear the questions he wanted to ask his father. But he was already gone, so she followed Margaret instead. Surely he'd fill her in on what they talked about on the way to the warehouse.

It wasn't exactly the way she wanted to partner with him, but for now, she'd bide her time. Damn, it was hard being patient, though. Why couldn't he treat her more like a partner? Or at least a trainee. She couldn't learn a damn thing sitting in the kitchen with his mother.

"Have a seat. How about something cold to drink?"

"No thank you," she said, casting furtive glances down the hall. It was already seven-thirty and in no time at all the shipment would arrive. She hoped Tyler's discussion with his father wouldn't take long. She was anxious to get out there and set up.

"Are you staying for dinner?" Margaret slid a casserole into the oven, then pulled up a chair at the kitchen table next to Nevada.

She shook her head. "I'm afraid we have other plans, but thanks for the invitation." What was keeping him?

"Tell me how things are going with you and Tyler. Getting along well?"

"Yes, as a matter of fact we are." She turned to Margaret, trying to give her undivided attention.

"Ah, yes, I can see that in your eyes."

"See what?"

"That look. You're in love with him."

How did mothers know so much? She smiled. "How can you tell?"

"I know that look, dear," Margaret said with a smile, patting her hand. "And like I told you before, he's in love with you."

There were so many things she wanted to talk to Margaret about, but now was not the time. She heard footsteps in the hall and turned to see Edward approaching.

Nevada looked around for Tyler, but didn't see him. "Is Tyler coming?"

Edward smiled indulgently and shook his head. "He left as soon as you two got here."

Her heart dropped to her feet. "Left?" She stood abruptly. "What do you mean left?"

When she would have taken off down the hall, Edward stopped her, gently grasping her arm. He shook his head. "He's already gone. Long gone. Said you were to stay here and he'd be back for you later."

"He what?!" How could he do this to her? Again! He left her again, just dumped her like an inconvenience to be dealt with later. "I don't understand. He was supposed to take me with him."

"He didn't explain to me, Nevada. Just said I was to keep you safe. You might as well relax and settle in. It could be a long night." He patted her hand like an indulgent father would a small child. She resisted the urge to pull her hand away, furious at the father as well as the son.

Long night, indeed. Sonofabitch! He'd never intended to take her with him. The firing lessons, the conversations and set up of the location, had all been a way to placate her into thinking she was going to help him. Goddamn him!

"Come, dear, sit down. Dinner will be ready soon."

"No, thank you, Margaret. I need to stand." She felt guilty over the biting words, but couldn't help it.

"You're angry with him, aren't you?"

"Beyond the ability to speak," she ground out. Her chest heaved with the effort to control her breathing as well as her anger. She wanted to scream, but knew it wouldn't do any good. And she had Margaret to consider.

"I'm sure he did this for your safety, Nevada," Margaret said, grasping her hand. "And I know you don't understand it now, but maybe he'll explain it when he gets back."

"Maybe." She'd never understand him. And he'd lied to her again! Fucking bastard! Her heart ached, her body shook with fury and pain and she wanted to scream loud enough to shake the chandelier. Damn him for doing this to her!

"He knows what he's doing. Don't worry about him. He'll be fine. Nothing you could do to help him anyway, so it's better you're out of his way." Edward's confident voice boomed through the kitchen.

Out of his way. That's what she was to Edward. In his son's way. Is that what Tyler thought too?

Margaret returned to her cooking and Nevada flopped in the kitchen chair, utterly defeated.

He'll explain it when he gets back. If he gets back. Warring with her anger was the overriding fear that he was going out to do this alone. Without her. Without backup.

She was devastated. He thought so little of her abilities to help him, he dumped her on his parents again.

Not this time. He *wasn't* going to do this alone. She couldn't allow it to happen. But she needed a plan. Tyler had already explained the advanced security system here, so just walking out the front door wasn't an option.

And if she knew Tyler, she also knew he'd briefed his father to hold her virtual prisoner here.

"If you don't mind, I'd like to go upstairs and lie down. I have a raging headache. Do you have some aspirin?" She backed away from the kitchen, working her way down the hall.

Margaret's face filled with concern. "Of course. Upstairs in the medicine cabinet of the guest bathroom. Go, lie down in Tyler's room."

"Thank you. And, I'm sorry, but I'm really not hungry at all, so don't wake me for dinner. I might just sleep all night."

Edward shot her a suspicious glance. Nevada prayed he fell for it. The last thing she needed was to have to outwit a military general. Damn Tyler for asking his father to babysit her.

"Are you all right?" Edward handed his empty glass to Margaret and turned to her.

Just how good an actress was she? She was about to find out. "It's my head," she said, trying to sound convincingly pained without being melodramatic. "Migraines. They come on me all of a sudden, usually in times of stress." She made a point to let her anger at Tyler show. "Forgive me, Edward, but your son stresses me."

That made Edward laugh, and she knew she'd convinced him. "I can understand that, my dear. But you know he's just trying to keep you safe."

"I know he is. Tell that to my head." She rubbed her temples. "If you'll excuse me, I think I'll just sleep this off."

"Good for you," Edward said. "We'll let Tyler know where you are when he returns."

She hated deceiving Margaret. But it couldn't be helped. She nodded and made her escape up the stairs.

Once she reached the safety of Tyler's room, she closed the door and bolted it shut, then hurried to the window and opened it as quietly as possible.

She had remembered correctly. There was a trellis right below the window. She'd already pulled Edward's keys from the kitchen counter and slipped them into her jeans pocket while Margaret's back was turned. As Tyler told her last time they visited, secondary access to the alarm system was located on Edward's key fob, and she pushed the button to disable the perimeter alarm.

Slipping the keys in her pocket, she started out the window, praying that the car keys attached to the key ring would fit Edward's car in the driveway.

Whether he knew it or not, whether he liked it or not, Tyler was going to have her help.

* * * * *

Tyler pulled out his cell phone and contemplated for the hundredth time that day whether or not to make the call. He was realistic enough to know the mission had a slim chance of succeeding without backup. He couldn't do it alone.

Now that he'd gotten Nevada safely ensconced in his parents' house, he could focus on bringing down the drug cartel. But that presented another problem. He needed help. But who? His gut told him he could trust Dylan, but what if he was wrong? He could compromise the entire mission as well as his own life.

"The hell with it," he murmured. His instincts had always been right before. He punched in a speed dial number.

"Yeah."

"Legend, it's Midnight."

"Midnight! Dammit, where the hell have you been?"

"Not now."

"Yeah, now. Is Velvet all right? Are you okay? We've been trying to get in touch with you. Goddamn, you had us worried. What the fuck is going on?"

"We're fine. But we've got trouble. I need you to meet me."

"Anything. Where?"

He gave Dylan a brief recap of what had happened and that he suspected someone in the Agency had sold him out. After he gave Dylan the location in code and that he needed to meet him as quickly as possible, he turned the car in the direction of the meeting spot, a location near the warehouse.

If his instincts were right, things with Dylan were on the up-and-up. He really needed an entire NCA squad for backup, but didn't have that choice.

His only other alternative would be going in by himself. That put the odds against him higher than he'd like. He'd feel much better with Dylan backing him up.

If Dylan was clean, that is. If he wasn't, the mission would be compromised.

And Tyler would be dead.

* * * * *

Nevada had never been more pissed off in her life. Anger bubbled up inside her and she wanted to smash something with her fists. That kind of reaction was unexpected, yet it also helped fuel her desire to get to Tyler.

First to help him. After that, she'd kill him.

Maybe killing was too strong a word. Maiming would be good. A well-placed kick to his balls, perhaps. Yes, that gave her a certain sense of satisfaction. The white-knuckled grip she had on the steering wheel lessened and she focused her attention on the road, forcing back the seething rage.

Use that anger on the bad guys, Nevada. There'll still be plenty left over for Tyler.

She checked her rearview mirror, then moved into the lane that would take her across the river to East St. Louis. Glancing at the clock on the dashboard, she realized she barely had time to make it before the scheduled delivery. Visions of Tyler trying to do this alone had her pulse racing. She wished she could call someone at the NCA, but she had no earthly idea who to trust.

Okay, so she wasn't the best backup Tyler could have, but she was better than nothing.

* * * * *

"See anything?"

"Not yet."

Tyler swore, hoping by now some of the major players would have arrived. He looked at his watch. Well after ten-thirty, the ten trucks arrived almost a half-hour ago. They'd positioned themselves behind the camouflaging brush at the top of a small hill in front of the warehouse.

He and Dylan lay on their stomachs watching the warehouse activities through their binoculars. Now that it was apparent Dylan could be trusted, he hoped the real NCA mole would show up.

"If somebody doesn't come soon, we'll have to go in and take the trucks and drivers and whoever's in charge. Even if they're not the big guns."

Tyler nodded. "I know. Just a few more minutes."

The larger trucks offloaded chemicals and equipment, transferring the drug-making supplies into smaller trucks. No doubt they'd be distributed throughout the region. Which meant, in less than a week, an incredible amount of meth would be available on the street.

But not if they could stop it. And they would stop it. Hopefully while doing so, he and Dylan would figure out who the mole was.

"Here comes a car." Tyler flattened himself into the tall grass and Dylan followed.

A black luxury sedan pulled into the entrance of the warehouse. Tyler lifted his binoculars and focused on the entering vehicle. "Looks like just one person driving."

"Recognize the person?"

"Not yet."

Tyler waited impatiently, anxious to get down there.

"Wait. They stopped just inside the door."

Drawing his binoculars, Tyler adjusted the lenses, then swore when he saw who exited the vehicle.

"Fuck!" Their job just got a helluva lot more complicated.

Dylan dropped the binoculars and looked over at Tyler. "The commander."

"Yeah." Disgust filled him. Commander Alan Webster had put both his and Nevada's life on the line. For what? Drugs? Big money?

His father wasn't such a good judge of character after all.

"You ready?" he asked Dylan, more determined than ever to bring the bastard into custody.

"Right behind you, partner."

The odds weren't good, but they weren't insurmountable, either. They carried enough firepower to take down everyone in that warehouse and only a handful were armed. The rest were most likely warehouse workers and wouldn't put up much of a fight. He and Dylan had gone over the plan. God willing, it would all go down fast and without a hitch.

Tyler was just thankful Nevada wasn't in the middle of all this. Worrying about her was a distraction he couldn't afford right now.

They crept down the hill, careful to stay low to the ground so they wouldn't be spotted. The commander was busy in conversation with a tall, thin man with long, stringy grey hair. They spoke together in rapid Spanish. Tyler would bet any money that was Mercado.

He stilled when the commander and Mercado moved, then exhaled when they stepped into the warehouse, the guards following. Tyler motioned to Dylan, who followed close behind him.

When they hit the tar of the road, they edged to the wide entrance, their bodies flattened against the side of the building. Tyler felt for his weapons, making sure they were securely strapped to the harness on his body. They wouldn't have time to search through a bag of goodies while trying to cover a half-dozen armed men, so they had to be loaded and locked, ready to fire.

Though he was hoping it wouldn't come to that.

They reached the entrance to the warehouse. Tyler saw the front of the two guards' feet hovering just inside the entrance.

It was go time. Thankful to have Dylan backing him up, he stepped into the doorway, automatic weapon drawn and pointed at the two guards. "Drop 'em," he whispered, his lowered voice indicating he wasn't going to ask more than once. The guards put their guns down and the warehouse went silent.

Dylan appeared next to him, his gaze trained on the armed men to the right, while Tyler focused on the left. They each had three men in their sights, all of whom pointed their weapons on both Tyler and Dylan.

"Looks like a stalemate to me."

Tyler froze at the familiar voice as a sharp, metal object poked him in the back. He didn't need to turn around to know who held a gun on him.

"Evening, Commander. Out to make a bust on your own tonight?"

Chapter Thirteen

ဢ

Nevada pulled her car into a space away from the warehouse, then gathered her bag and trudged up the hill overlooking the area. When she reached the top, she dropped to a crawl and skimmed her way to the rise.

Grabbing for her binoculars, she focused on the wide entrance. Lights were blazing. Several trucks were parked just inside the warehouse. A flurry of activity surrounded her. She counted around a dozen men, at least seven or eight of them with guns.

Training her binoculars just to the left of the doorway, her breath caught as she spied Tyler and Legend, their hands in the air, and three men with assault weapons pushing them into the warehouse. Standing smugly at the entrance doorway was Commander Webster!

She laid her forehead on the cool grass, focusing on keeping her breathing in check. The urge to hyperventilate and panic was strong and she had to fight it back. This was gut check time. If she ever wanted to be a field agent she had to learn to act cool in a crisis. And this was as close to a crisis as she would probably ever come.

What to do? Going in there on her own would be stupid. Tyler and Legend had been taken, and they were experienced agents. She hadn't even started her training program, and other than rudimentary skills with a gun and a few of the high-powered rifles, her rushing in there to defend them would be like tossing a snowball into a volcano—useless.

It was obvious that Commander Webster was the NCA mole, but what if there were others? Contacting anyone there, even the assistant commander, could be dangerous.

Which left her with only one option. She didn't like the idea, but she had no choice. There was only one person she knew she could trust.

She flipped over onto her back and grabbed the bag, searching and finding the cell phone Tyler had given her. She turned it on, hoping like hell that she could get Tyler and Legend some help quickly.

The phone rang once, twice, three times. With each ring she prayed for an answer.

When she heard the voice on the other line, she breathed a sigh of relief and readied herself for some fast and furious explanations.

"This is Nevada. Don't say a word. I need your help quick!"

* * * * *

This was one fine fucking mess. Tyler grimaced as the rope cut into his wrist. Trying to struggle to loosen the thick twine binding him wasn't doing any good. He struggled to a sitting position, trying to gauge everyone's whereabouts.

The cement floor was cold and filthy, smelling like oil spills and chemicals.

At least they were still alive, which led Tyler to believe that he and Dylan were being saved to use as bargaining chips. Mercado and Webster had called for reinforcements, too. Now about twenty men milled around, unloading semi-trailers and reloading smaller trucks. Clangs and clatters ricocheted through the warehouse like metal on metal. It had to be the meth chemicals and supplies.

None of the men were NCA, thankfully. Maybe the mole was limited to one person. Commander Webster sure as hell had all the information he'd ever need at his disposal. Every code he'd given to Nevada, every detail of his work on this case had been read and analyzed by the commander. No wonder he'd never made any headway. Webster had let him take two steps forward and then one step back, making him feel like he was inching his way toward discovery of the kingpins of this operation, only to snatch the rug out from under him and make him work harder than ever.

Carrot on a string, he thought with ironic amusement. He laughed.

"Okay, I give up. You tell me what's so fucking funny about this."

Tyler looked over at Dylan and shrugged. "The way Webster played me on this assignment."

"Oh, hell. None of us knew he was in on this. Webster's a decorated veteran, for Christ's sake. Who would ever suspect him?"

Tyler hadn't. Nor had his own father and his father wasn't a stupid man. In fact, Webster probably would have gotten away with it if it hadn't been for Nevada's skills in discovering Mercado's link to the meth production lab. She'd been the one to break the case, a fact not lost on him at the moment.

He hoped he'd live long enough to thank her.

As far as his father, he'd be crushed to learn of Webster's betrayal. Though he might disagree with his dad's philosophy on life, he could sure use his help about now. The only relief he felt was knowing that Nevada was safe. If she'd come with him on this assignment, she'd have been caught and facing death like him, or even worse. Bad enough he'd involved Dylan in all this.

"Got any brilliant ideas?" Dylan whispered.

"Not at the moment." But he sure as hell wasn't going to sit idly by and wait for Webster and Mercado to decide what to do with them. The two men had their heads buried together, whispering. Webster occasionally glanced over at Tyler with a concerned frown.

Or was that regret? Did Webster have a conscience after all? The two men finally left, entering a door marked "Office" at the back of the warehouse. The guards were busy watching the workers load the trucks, which meant no one watched him and Dylan right now.

Tyler moved his hands and felt behind him for anything that could cut the ropes. He twisted his head around as far as he could, spotting several wood pallets about six feet behind them. The wood had sharp points at the edges. It might work.

He scooted slowly to avoid catching the guard's attention. Dylan watched, then moved with him. Soon they were backed against the pallets, keeping their eyes on the guards while rubbing the ropes against the sharp edges of the pallets.

Miracle of miracles, the ropes began to loosen. Tyler winced at the raw, burning pain and the warm wetness of blood at his wrists, knowing he was also scratching gouges into his skin, but that didn't matter right now. Getting free was the only priority.

He finally broke through the ropes, shaking them off his wrists but keeping his hands behind his back. He looked over at Dylan, who was close to doing the same. Dylan had just broken free of the ropes when a commotion sounded outside. The guards went running and Webster and Mercado came flying through the office door, guns drawn.

Webster cast a quick look in their direction before heading to the doorway, crouching low behind some barrels.

"This is the NCA! The warehouse is surrounded. Drop your weapons and surrender!"

Tyler exhaled a sigh of relief. The good guys had arrived! How, he didn't know. Maybe someone else on the inside knew about Webster. Right now he didn't care. He smelled a rescue.

"Get ready to move," he whispered to Dylan, who nodded.

Tyler moved into a crouch and started inching toward the guards on their side of the warehouse. Hiding behind the cover of the trucks allowed them to sneak close to the two guards. Everyone's attention was on the outside of the warehouse. Even Webster and Mercado hadn't looked in their direction.

In an instant Tyler and Dylan had silently dispatched the guards, grabbing their automatic weapons. Tyler pointed to Dylan, telling him without words to circle around the farthest truck.

After Dylan disappeared, Tyler crept toward Webster's location. Fucking coward stood at the back of the guards, hiding behind the burly men. Mercado was on the other side of the doorway, doing the same thing.

He smirked, assuming to be a bigwig in this type of operation meant you got to get shot last. He spotted Dylan circling around the side of the farthest truck, inching up behind Mercado. Tyler signaled him, letting him know what he was going to do. Dylan nodded, a lethal smile appearing on his lips.

There was so much noise from the helicopters outside that Webster didn't even hear him approach. He reached around the commander, wrapping his forearm around the man's throat and driving the barrel of the weapon into his back. "Looks like a stalemate to me," he whispered into the commander's ear, using the man's earlier words.

Webster stiffened, his gaze shooting toward Mercado. Dylan had Mercado in the same hold, gun pointed at his back.

Tyler and Dylan moved to the back and to the center of the guards surrounding them. The guards looked confused, their gazes darting outside and back at their leaders.

"Hell of a dilemma, isn't it, guys? Protect these two or worry about the NCA outside? I'd say you're fucked either way. If you're smart, you'll lay down right now while you can still breathe."

"Don't listen to him," Webster said. "He's bluffing."

"You almost got me and Velvet killed, asshole," Tyler ground out. "You've betrayed your country and your agents' trust. I wouldn't be taking any bets that you'll live through this."

Tyler realized he was looking for an excuse to gun the bastard down. "Go ahead, Webster. Flinch. Just a little. I'll blow a hole through your belly so wide that you could toss a football through it."

Webster froze, sweat trickling down his face and neck and dropping onto Tyler's forearm. Tyler grinned.

By the time the confused guards turned around to survey the outside situation, they were faced with over two dozen armed NCA agents. Weapons dropped to the concrete faster than lightning striking the ground.

"Looks like it's prison time for you and your friend, Mercado," Tyler said, pushing Webster toward the NCA assistant commander, Rufus Sanders. A rugged-looking mountain man in his early fifties, Sanders was not someone Tyler would ever want to fuck with. He was old-time military and also a good friend of Tyler's dad.

"Commander," Tyler nodded, pushing Webster closer.

Sanders nodded and smiled. "Well done, men." Turning to the other agents, he said, "Take this scum out of my sight. The United States government is going to want to have a very long talk with the ex-commander of the NCA."

After Webster and Mercado and the others were led away, Sanders grinned, hands on his hips. "What a fucking mess."

Tyler rubbed the raw skin of his wrists and nodded. "A major clusterfuck, sir."

Sanders jammed his fingers through his thinning brown hair. "You can say that again. Thank God your father contacted us or you two could be dead meat by now."

His father?

"Sir? Did you say my father?"

"Yeah. He called me at home after he was alerted by your trainee."

"Uh, trainee, sir?"

"Yes. Your trainee."

Tyler's gaze whipped around Sanders.

Nevada. What the hell was she doing here?

"Ne…Agent Velvet, what are you doing here?"

"Just following orders…sir," she shot back, anger turning her eyes dark. "When you left me behind for…watch duty, I saw you and Agent Legend captured. Realizing Commander Webster was the NCA mole, I didn't know who to trust, so I contacted your father since I knew he had military and intelligence connections. Fortunately he called Commander Sanders, here, and they met me on the slope outside."

Somehow he knew he was being spared her tirade because of NCA protocol. Sonofabitch. She was covering his ass in front of the commander! "Well done, Agent Velvet," he said, at a loss for words.

Dylan snorted and when Tyler shot him a glare, scratched his nose, winked and stepped outside.

"You all did a fine job. Agent Velvet, you are one hell of a trainee. Quick and smart thinking on your part." Sanders patted her shoulder and followed Dylan out, leaving Tyler alone with Nevada.

She'd saved his ass. His and Dylan's. "How did you manage to get out of my father's house?"

She arched a brow. "I'm resourceful. Not that you'd ever give me credit for it."

Ouch. "Nevada, I was only trying to protect you."

Her anger was palpable, emanating off her like heat from a roaring campfire. "Bullshit. You don't trust me. You think I'm incompetent." Before he could answer she hefted the bag of weapons he'd given her and shoved it into his stomach, momentarily rendering him incapable of speech.

He struggled past the loss of breath and said, "Nevada, you have to understand…"

She cut him off with a wave of her hand. "No, you need to understand exactly how I feel. You are one arrogant prick, Tyler Call. Your lack of faith in me made me realize that training under you would be a colossal career mistake. Monday morning, I'm asking for a transfer to another training agent."

"Training? I think we have a lot more together than just our mutual profession."

She got into his face, leaning close enough that he could smell her sweet scent. "Whatever we once had is over. Got that? I couldn't possibly have a relationship with someone who thinks so little of my intelligence." For emphasis, she jammed her finger in his chest. "Don't you ever fucking come near me again. If you do, I'll show you how goddamned resourceful I can really be!"

She turned on her heel and stormed out, leaving him alone in a warehouse that had just grown very, very cold.

* * * * *

Nevada bent over and rested her hands on her knees, watching the droplets of sweat drip off her face and arms. She struggled for breath. The only thing keeping her standing right now was the abject embarrassment she'd feel if she passed out in front of her training officer.

Dylan stopped next to her and patted her on the back. "You okay, Velvet?"

For two grueling weeks he'd punished her mercilessly, making her memorize the agent manual so he could quiz her. Then he'd force her to run these damn marathon-like sprints and climb over walls and through netting until she wanted to strangle him. Or throw up. Or both. "I'm fine."

At least the physical exertion served as an outlet for her emotions. It was only on her off time that she curled up into a ball and let the tears fall, regretting all that she'd lost.

Or all she'd never had.

Dammit, she missed Tyler. Hated him, but missed him, too.

Legend's grueling training at least served one purpose. Lately she'd fallen into bed and passed right out after a day with him.

But it didn't keep Tyler from entering her dreams. Her body woke sweating and aroused after a night spent in the arms of a man who would forever be just a fantasy.

"Come on, Velvet, that wasn't hard at all. Besides, your stamina is increasing every day."

"You're some kind of inhuman machine, Legend. Nobody could have that much energy."

He laughed and clapped her on the back, nearly knocking her over. She struggled to keep her legs from trembling.

"Okay, you've had enough for today. Let's go get cleaned up and I'll buy you a beer."

Right now she'd drink anything as long as it was cold and didn't require running or climbing anything to get it. They walked back to the NCA training center. Nevada showered and dressed, knowing her muscles would be screaming at her tomorrow morning.

And she wanted to be an agent? Was she insane?

None of this was any fun without Tyler. She hated that most of all.

Time to buck it up and get on with your life. You two are finished and you've got a career to think of.

She followed Legend to a little spaghetti place known as the hangout for a lot of the NCA agents. They waved to their peers and grabbed a table at the back of the room. The waitress brought them two chilled mugs of beer and Nevada drank it down like a glass of cold water.

"Thirsty?" he asked, arching a brow at her.

Anyone would be thrilled to have Dylan as a partner. Smart, resourceful, funny as hell and not damn bad to look at either.

But he's not Tyler.

Shut up, voice.

"Midnight's quit the NCA," Dylan announced.

Her gaze shot up from the menu and met his. "What?"

"He quit. Last week. Turned in his notice and just dropped out."

Don't ask. Don't care. "Why?"

Dammit!

Dylan shrugged. "Said it wasn't what he wanted to do the rest of his life. That he had other plans now."

What other plans? *No, don't ask!* "What other plans?"

Shit!

"I guess you'd have to ask him if you're interested."

"I'm not."

"Uh-huh."

"I'm not!"

Dylan took a long swallow of his beer and set the mug down, leaning toward her so that only she could hear him. "I hate to inform you of this, but Tyler is a man."

Didn't she know it. "Your point?"

"We're stupid when it comes to women. Make all the wrong choices and screw up all the time. It takes a strong woman to realize that her man can piss her off enough to think murderous thoughts but also realize that he loves her like crazy."

"He doesn't love me." When Dylan didn't respond, she said it again. "He doesn't!"

"Yeah, he does. But that's your choice to make and nobody else's. I can only tell you what I know."

"Which is?" Why did she keep asking? She didn't want to know anything about Tyler. Ever.

"That I've never seen him act the way he did when he was around you. To him, an agent was an agent. Male or female, they got treated the same. He didn't treat you like an agent."

"I know." And that was the problem.

"But can you really blame him, Nev? He didn't treat you like an agent because he was too busy treating you like a woman. Like *his* woman."

Nevada couldn't get Dylan's words out of her mind all through dinner. Right now she could barely keep her thoughts on the road. When her car found itself outside Tyler's condo, she wasn't surprised.

I don't care about him. I just need to know, that's all.

She took the elevator up and stood at his door for a full five minutes before ringing the bell.

"It's open!" he shouted.

Oh, God. What if he was expecting a date?

So what? You're not together anymore. If he's got a woman coming over, who cares?

She did, that's who. Turning the knob, she opened the door a little, expecting to see his dining room table candlelit with plates for two.

"Money's on the table. Just leave the pizza there. There's extra for the tip, Joe. Thanks!"

Pizza. Her breath expelled in a whoosh of relief as she realized he'd been expecting pizza delivery. In fact, a teenager appeared right behind her with a square box in his hand.

Nevada grabbed the money on the table, paid the boy and closed the door, inhaling the sweet smell of pepperoni. She hadn't even touched her dinner with Dylan and her stomach was complaining rather loudly about it right now.

Okay, this was awkward. She set the pizza on the table and stood inside the door, not knowing what to do.

When Tyler whipped around the corner and stopped dead in his tracks, eyes wide, she realized she'd just made a huge mistake.

Freshly showered, his tight abs showcased by his shirtless upper half, she forgot how to breathe. He wore only jeans, half-zipped. The soft, dark down covering his lower abdomen trailed enticingly into his jeans.

And she was intimately familiar with where it trailed to.

"Nevada."

She swallowed. "Tyler."

"I've tried to call you. To see you."

"I know." She hadn't answered her phone or her door, knowing it was him.

"What are you doing here?"

She had no idea. What *was* she doing here? "I...I..." *Think fast. That's your job, remember?* "I paid the pizza boy."

She cringed. Brilliant.

He regarded her warily. "Uhh, thanks. Would you like some?"

No. She was leaving. "Yes, I'm starving."

Oh, God, she was suffering from multiple personality disorder.

Like a mute she followed him into the kitchen as he grabbed paper plates and tossed them down on the table. He opened the pizza and laid out a thick, juicy slice on her plate.

Instead of speaking, she laid into her pizza like she hadn't eaten in a week. Surprisingly, the silence between them wasn't uncomfortable. He opened two sodas and handed her one, which she accepted with a mouth-filled nod.

Finally satiated, she wiped her mouth with the napkin, determined to get some answers and then get the hell out of his condo.

And his life.

"Dylan told me you quit the NCA."

"Yeah."

"Why?"

He stood and emptied their plates into the trash, grabbing another soda and leaning against the counter. "Let's just said I had an epiphany."

"What kind of epiphany?"

His smile didn't reach his eyes. "Actually, some of it came about because of you."

"Me? I don't understand."

Pushing away from the counter, he walked toward her and crouched down in front of her. She inhaled that soap-clean smell that reminded her so much of him it made her heart ache.

"I fell in love with you, Nevada. I know I handled a lot of things badly with you, but it was like I couldn't separate the agent in you from the woman in you. I fell in love with Nevada, not with Velvet. I tried to protect Nevada, not Velvet."

Which is what Dylan had told her. Surprisingly, she began to understand. "But why did you quit the agency?"

"I had a revelation of sorts while working with my dad on this case and I suddenly realized I don't want to be like my father. I don't want to be gone all the time, risking my life and leaving behind a wife and children who'll someday look at me like I'm a stranger."

"What does that have to do with me?"

He reached for her hands. "You were the wife I was thinking of. You're the woman I love."

She sucked in a breath, her stomach flipping like crazy.

"You're also the agent I should have allowed to back me up on the raid on the warehouse. But honest to God, Nevada, the thought of risking your life made my gut hurt. I made a decision to protect you, instead of trusting you and talking it over with you. In the end, you came through. I fucked up and lost you."

"Yes, Tyler, you did fuck up. I'd make a damn good agent."

He smiled. "I know."

"But you didn't lose me." The realization hit her as soon as the words spilled from her lips. She was still angry as hell at him, but it didn't change the fact she loved him. And now it was time to take that leap she'd been so afraid of before. "I love you, Tyler Call. You infuriate me, but I love you."

He stood and hauled her to her feet, pulling her against him. His heart pounded as quickly as hers.

"I need to ask you something. I'm not very good at this so I'm going to screw it up, but here goes."

Oh, God.

"I promise to love you, be there for you and protect you every day for the rest of our lives. Marry me, Nevada."

"What?" She needed a paper bag. This was too much. She was hyperventilating, her breaths coming in short, quick gasps.

"You heard me. Marry me. Be my wife and my partner."

"Partner?"

"I'm opening a private investigation firm. Nothing fancy like NCA stuff, so if you still want to go the agent route I'll understand. Your professional choices are up to you."

What *did* she want?

It didn't take her long to realize that the adventure she craved could be found in the arms of the man she loved. That she hated NCA agent field training because Tyler wasn't with her. It was like her personal and professional life centered around him, and she'd never be happy unless she could have both.

She felt like she was balancing on the precipice and only she could decide which way to jump. She looked to her past, to all she missed out on because of her irrational fears, and knew there was only one choice to make.

She cradled his face in her hands and pressed a kiss to his lips. "I love you, Tyler. I'd love to be your wife."

He grinned like a child on Christmas morning. "And my partner in Call & Call Investigations?"

"Call and Call, huh? How about Call 'n James?"

He raised a brow. "Oh, so you're turning down my marriage proposal?"

She wrinkled her nose at him. "No, dumbass. Just trying to establish the parameters of our business relationship."

"I see." His look was all business, but she caught the gleam in his eyes. "Call 'n James, huh? How about CNJ Investigations, then?"

She laughed with pure joy. "CNJ. Simple. I like it. Okay, partner, it's a deal. As long as you let me do the research. You're too grouchy with the computer."

"Me? Grouchy? I think it's you who's grouchy. Especially on the computer."

She could already tell they'd do battle. And often. She wouldn't want it any other way. "And the legwork we can do together." Just the thought of working with him again sent her adrenaline pumping.

He pressed his lips against hers in a kiss that spoke from his heart and brought tears to her eyes. "Thank you for calling my dad. You saved our lives."

"You're welcome."

"You were probably pissed as hell that I dumped you at my parents."

She leveled a stern glare at him. "You're damn right I was. But I managed to escape. No easy feat with your father's security and eagle eye."

He laughed. "I knew you were good, Agent Velvet."

"Oh, but I can be better, Agent Midnight. With the right kind of training."

"Is that right?" His hands slid behind her back, reaching down to cup her buttocks and pull her intimately against him. "I love training."

"Mm, so do I." She rocked against his hard cock. God, she'd missed being close to him. He thrust against her palm, making her knees weak.

"Good." His voice lowered to that husky tone she'd fallen in love with the first time she'd heard him on the phone. "First lesson: on your knees."

She threw her head back and laughed, then nodded. "Of course. You're the training agent." She dropped to her knees, keeping her gaze focused on his as she drew the zipper the rest of the way down, jerking his jeans to his knees.

Tyler sucked in a breath, his eyes black with his desire.

"What next?" she asked innocently.

"Suck me."

"I'll do my best." She cradled the twin sacs under his cock within her hands and caressed them as she stroked his shaft with the other, then covered the head with her lips, drawing him inside the heat of her mouth.

Tyler groaned and fisted his hand in her hair, pumping his shaft in and out of her mouth in a slow, erotic rhythm that made her panties wet with her own need.

"I'll bet you want my tongue on your pussy, don't you?" he asked, his voice tight and strained.

She stood when he held out his hand for her. "Yes, I do."

He stripped off his jeans and lifted her, carrying her into the bedroom, pulling at her clothes quickly until she was naked. He crawled onto the bed, caressing her from ankles to thighs and stopping between her outstretched legs. "I'll want lots of sex, Nevada. I hope you're up to the task because I can't seem to get enough of you."

As she watched him bend and settle his mouth near her aching pussy, she smiled. "I think I can handle that."

He blew a soft, warm breath against the dark curls of her mound. "Even at the office we set up together. Think you can handle being fucked by your partner?"

"Mmm," she said, reaching for his head to thread her fingers through his dark locks. "I think I can definitely handle that."

He took one long swipe of her slit and she arched her hips, crying out at the exquisite sensation of his hot tongue on her throbbing flesh. "Every day. Whenever I want you. I have this vision of putting you on your back on my desk, then spreading your legs and standing between them, fucking you until you scream."

She closed her eyes and imaged the thrill of working with him, loving him, every day spent together. "No secretary, then."

"And an office with soundproof walls." He fit his mouth around her clit and sucked; at the same time, he slipped his fingers inside her and pumped. Nevada shrieked and flooded his hand with her orgasm.

Moving up her body, he pressed his lips against hers, giving her a taste of her own juices, making her crave the joining between them. He filled his hands with her breasts, squeezing them together and licking the nipples until they stood hard and erect, glistening with his saliva.

"Tyler, please."

"I love it when you beg for my cock, baby. You gonna do that every day for me?"

How could she not, when she wanted him desperately? She couldn't imagine a day going by when she wouldn't crave the feel of his hard shaft inside her, creating a joining that she had only dreamed existed.

"You know I will. I need you inside me. Quit fucking around and fuck me."

He threw his head back and laughed, then took her mouth in a ravaging kiss that spoke volumes without words. He slid effortlessly inside her and thrust slow and easy, taking her ever higher into a madness of desire.

"Harder," she urged.

"Not yet."

"Faster."

"Soon," he teased, making her crazy until she nipped at his bottom lip and dug her nails into his back. She lifted her hips, grinding against him until he stopped playing with her.

Tyler slammed her down onto the mattress and cupped her buttocks, drawing her as close as he could, then fucked her furiously until she was drenched in sweat and screaming his name, poised on the pinnacle of an earth-shattering orgasm.

He didn't skip a beat as he rolled her over so that she was on top.

"Finish us off," he commanded.

She reached for the headboard and pushed off, sliding over his cock, then rocking against him until she splintered inside, a crashing orgasm sending her juices pouring over him. He gripped her hips and moved her faster against him, drawing out that agonizing need again until she screamed his name and he came with her, flooding her with his cum.

She fell onto his chest and listened to his heart beat rapidly, then gradually slow. Twining her fingers through the hairs of his chest, she was more content than she'd ever been before.

She loved this man with all her heart. Before, the thought would have frightened her. Now she welcomed the unknown tomorrow. If she had a day, or fifty years with Tyler, it would be enough.

Nevada had never felt more sure of anything, more comfortable with giving up control and taking risks. Tyler was right. She couldn't control her life or his, but she was willing to risk her heart.

It may have taken her awhile to figure it out, but it finally came to her as the man she loved kissed her deeply and rolled her onto her back.

"Lesson two," he said, arching one wicked brow.

Ah, yes, Much better than a fantasy over the telephone. Real love like this was worth any risk.

Her eyes adjusting to the darkness, Starr could make out faint shapes in the room. Why was she in this room, not even chained, instead of their prison? None of this made sense, but she wasn't going to stay here long enough to find the answers.

She'd kill whoever got in her way, but she'd make her way back to Dognelle tonight.

Starr spied a tall vase sitting on a pedestal, and shuffled slowly toward it, her toes sinking into the thick rug in front of the bed. Her fingers closed over the bottom of the vase and she lifted it.

Heavy. Perfect to clout a hulking Raynar over the head.

She froze at the sound of creaking floorboards in the next room. A light shone through the crack in the door. Starr hurried into position next to the door, hoping that whoever came through didn't see her lurking there before she had the chance to split their skull.

The light brightened as the door opened, and she hefted the object, prepared to strike.

Suddenly the vase was pulled from her hands and a pair of strong arms circled her waist, squeezing the breath out of her. The stranger pulled her against his massive chest and she was roughly pulled through the doorway. She squinted in the bright lights, trying to fight off whoever had a death grip around her middle.

"Let go of me, you barbarian! I can't breathe!"

He whipped her around so her back rested against his chest. "Good. Now listen to me," he whispered, his breath warm against her cheek.

"You have nothing to say that I'd be interested in hearing." She leaned as far forward as possible, giving her leverage to kick her foot up to smash against his balls. But he countered by shoving one strong thigh between her legs.

She struggled, and she was by no means physically weak. But her strength was no match for the Raynar warrior. Finally, she gave up, sucking in a huge gulp of air when he relaxed his grip. He turned her around and held on to her shoulders. She glanced up and finally got a good look at the beast who held her.

Only he was no beast. Broad shoulders were centered by a wide chest covered in a dusting of dark hair. His narrow waist and slender hips rested on well-muscled thighs encased in very tight leather breeches. He was so tall she had to tilt her head back to see his face.

Brilliant blue eyes shone from sun-darkened skin. Raven black hair surrounded his face.

By Lal's halos, he was gorgeous.

While she was filthy and smelled like *balon* shit. And why the hell did she care? She never noticed men, didn't care for them, had never had a man and had no intention of lying down with this one.

Clearly, she'd suffered a head injury of sorts. What else would make her react this way to the heathen in front of her?

"Are you quite though ogling me?" he asked, amusement dancing in his wicked smile.

"I never ogle," she said. Not until just now, anyway.

He let go of her arms and walked over to a table against the wall. She eyed him warily while plotting her escape through the double doors on the other side of the room.

"Don't bother," he said nonchalantly, his back still turned to her. "There are guards on the other side of the door."

"Do you read minds?"

"No. You're just obvious."

Bastard.

He turned and approached her, holding out a cup. "Drink this."

"Fuck you."

"Not for a Kingdom's jewels. You stink."

Heat rose from her neck to her cheeks and she was thankful for the dirt covering her face. She couldn't even tell him he smelled just as bad because he'd obviously bathed. "Sorry, I haven't had time to primp in advance of our meeting," was all she could manage.

One corner of his mouth lifted. "Drink this. It's water. The physician said you suffered a head injury and you were to drink water when you woke."

She eyed the glass suspiciously. No way was she going to drink some liquid that could be poison.

Until he took a sip, then held it out to her. She licked her lips, barely able to swallow from the grit scratching her throat. The urge to take the glass from his hands and gulp down its contents was nearly overwhelming, but she'd be damned if she'd accept anything from him. "I don't want any."

He shrugged and set the glass on a table next to them. "Suit yourself."

She was dying for a drink, nearly ready to pass out from the thirst, but she'd never show weakness to this barbarian.

"I've also ordered a bath for you."

He walked toward the door and opened it, whispering something to the guard standing there. While his back was turned she grabbed the glass, gulping the liquid so quickly some of it dribbled down her chin.

A bath. She'd give her right arm for a bath right now. "I don't need a bath."

He closed the door, then walked toward her again, stopping inches away from her. Arching a brow, he sniffed loudly. "Oh, hell yes you do."

Well aware of how she smelled, she crossed her arms, defiantly lifting her chin. "You can't force me to bathe."

His height towered over hers. She'd never considered herself small. But next to this warrior, she felt like a child.

"I can force you to do whatever I want you to, and you will obey."

She sneered at him. "Perhaps you've mistaken me for one of your concubines. I am a free woman, not a slave."

"Not any longer. You are in the Raynar kingdom now, and as a female that puts you under our protection. Whatever freedoms you enjoyed before are gone."

She pushed aside the fear that knifed through her at the thought of her freedom being taken away. "Then run me through now. I'd rather be dead than be a slave to any man."

He tipped her chin with his finger. She refused to pull away, daring him to treat her like one of the many concubines known to exist in this kingdom. "What is your name, woman?" he asked.

"My name is Starr, and I am Queen of Dognelle. You will return me at once to my people."

His eyes widened for a moment, and then he laughed. "You are no queen. No leader of people could be a slight little girl with more dirt than weight on her."

This lower than scum warrior would definitely have to die. And soon. "Bring me before your king. I want to discuss terms of my release."

The tall warrior's eyes narrowed and he crossed his arms, widening his stance. The position made him appear all the more imposing.

"I am Lycan, King of Raynar, and there will be no discussion of your release. You are my captive, my slave, and I'll do whatever I wish with you."

Starr let her eyes drift shut for a second, praying to the gods that this wasn't true. This man, this savage, lived a comfortable life behind his opulent walls while the people of Dognelle went hungry. Ending his life would be her greatest wish.

About the Author

ဿ

In April 2003, Ellora's Cave foolishly offered me a contract for my first erotic romance and I haven't shut up since. My writing is an addiction for which there is no cure, a disease in which strange characters live in my mind, all clamoring for their own story. I try to let them out one by one, as mixing snarling werewolves with a bondage and discipline master can be very dangerous territory. Then again, unusual plotlines offer relief from the demons plaguing me.

In my world, well-endowed, naked cabana boys do the vacuuming and dishes, little faeries flit about dusting the furniture and doing laundry, Wolfgang Puck fixes my dinner and I spend every night engaged in wild sexual abandon with a hunky alpha. Okay, the hunky alpha part is my real life husband and he keeps my fantasy life enriched with extensive "research". But Wolfgang won't answer my calls, the faeries are on strike and my readers keep running off with the cabana boys.

Jaci welcomes comments from readers. You can find her website and email address on her author bio page at www.ellorascave.com.

Why an electronic book?

We live in the Information Age—an exciting time in the history of human civilization in which technology rules supreme and continues to progress in leaps and bounds every minute of every hour of every day. For a multitude of reasons, more and more avid literary fans are opting to purchase e-books instead of paperbacks. The question to those not yet initiated to the world of electronic reading is simply: *why?*

1. *Price.* An electronic title at Ellora's Cave Publishing and Cerridwen Press runs anywhere from 40-75% less than the cover price of the <u>exact same title</u> in paperback format. Why? Cold mathematics. It is less expensive to publish an e-book than it is to publish a paperback, so the savings are passed along to the consumer.

2. *Space.* Running out of room to house your paperback books? That is one worry you will never have with electronic novels. For a low one-time cost, you can purchase a handheld computer designed specifically for e-reading purposes. Many e-readers are larger than the average handheld, giving you plenty of screen room. Better yet, hundreds of titles can be stored within your new library—a single microchip. (Please note that Ellora's Cave and Cerridwen Press does not endorse any specific brands. You can check our website at www.ellorascave.com or

www.cerridwenpress.com for customer recommendations we make available to new consumers.)

3. *Mobility*. Because your new library now consists of only a microchip, your entire cache of books can be taken with you wherever you go.

4. *Personal preferences are accounted for*. Are the words you are currently reading too small? Too large? Too...**ANNOYING**? Paperback books cannot be modified according to personal preferences, but e-books can.

5. *Instant gratification*. Is it the middle of the night and all the bookstores are closed? Are you tired of waiting days—sometimes weeks—for online and offline bookstores to ship the novels you bought? Ellora's Cave Publishing sells instantaneous downloads 24 hours a day, 7 days a week, 365 days a year. Our e-book delivery system is 100% automated, meaning your order is filled as soon as you pay for it.

Those are a few of the top reasons why electronic novels are displacing paperbacks for many an avid reader. As always, Ellora's Cave and Cerridwen Press welcomes your questions and comments. We invite you to email us at service@ellorascave.com, service@cerridwenpress.com or write to us directly at: 1056 Home Ave. Akron OH 44310-3502.

Discover for yourself why readers can't get enough of the multiple award-winning publisher Ellora's Cave. Whether you prefer e-books or paperbacks, be sure to visit EC on the web at www.ellorascave.com for an erotic reading experience that will leave you breathless.

www.ellorascave.com